KADE'S Return

USA TODAY BESTSELLING AUTHOR

HEATHER SLADE

A complete list of Heather Slade's
series and titles is available at
the end of this book or
visit her website:
HEATHERSLADE.COM

Table of Contents

1

Kade

He'd been waiting over twenty years to be close enough to kill the man who'd ripped to shreds the life of a woman Kade had loved. Finally, he was able to avenge the horrors she'd faced the day Rory Calder raped and left her for dead. He'd almost killed him then, but Leech Hess, the woman's father, had stopped him. He wondered if Leech also regretted that Kade didn't get the shot off.

As he walked out from the shadows, he came face-to-face with a different woman. The last time he'd talked to her in person, she was a little girl. Between then and now, he'd only watched her from afar, although there hadn't been a single day when he didn't think about her, worry about her, or pray he did right by her.

"Let's get one thing straight, Eighty-eight," Kade said to the man to whom he'd entrusted her safety, Mercer Bryant. "She never was his daughter. She's always been mine."

Kade walked over and cupped her cheek with the palm of his hand. "Hello, Quinn," he said.

Mercer let her go, and Kade held her in his arms for the first time in fourteen years.

"Hi," she murmured, burying her face in his shoulder. "I remember you," she whispered.

"I'm so happy you do."

"Are you really my father?"

He understood why she'd asked. When he'd crept in the back door of the building where she was being held with a gun to her head, Kade overheard Mercer tell Calder, the man threatening to kill her, that he wouldn't do it, because Quinn was his flesh and blood. Moments later, Kade had contradicted that by saying she was his daughter.

"Welcome home, son," said his father, who Mercer had untied and helped to his feet.

Kade let go of Quinn and walked over to embrace his da, whose eyes filled with tears.

He took a step back and looked him over. "What did Calder do to you?" Kade asked.

"Knocked me out with something. I don't remember much," his father answered.

Laird Butler, retired intelligence agent, code name Burns, had always been his oldest son's hero—today more than ever. At seventy years old, he was still as fit and strong as men half his age.

Showing emotion was something trained out of people in their line of work, but Kade couldn't deny the feelings seeing his father invoked any more than Laird was able to.

"We should get Burns, Quinn, and Monk checked out," suggested Mercer.

"Good idea, Eighty-eight." Kade looked over to the other side of the building, where Mantis and Dutch had untied Monk. Another man lay face down in a pool of blood. "Who's that?"

"Max Lista," Mercer answered. "Our hire but, evidently, working with Calder in some capacity."

Later, Kade would discuss the breach with him and their two other partners in K19 Security Solutions, Paps and Razor. He looked at Quinn, who stood with Mercer's arm around her shoulders. She was studying him.

"You're safe now," he said, walking closer to her. Kade knew she was waiting for an answer to her question about whether he was her father or not, and soon, he'd give it to her. But not here, not surrounded by death and evil. "Let's get you out of here," he said instead. "I'll have Mercer take you to see my ma," he added. "Da, you go with them."

While Kade was a trained physician's assistant, he had fallout to deal with here and wouldn't feel comfortable examining either Quinn or his father in this setting.

Mantis and Dutch, both K19 operatives, would supervise the rest of the team who were making their way into the building to remove all traces of evidence of what had gone down in the last hour. They'd need a sweep and clean crew in here as soon as possible too.

"Should we take that one, Doc?" Dutch asked, pointing at Max Lista's body.

Kade nodded. It was Calder's body he was more concerned about. He'd made a deal he intended to make good on.

"I'll gather the family," said Laird.

"Not today, Da." Kade motioned in Quinn's direction. "I need some time."

"Sorcha will meet us at the Harmony house," Mercer told them.

As far as his siblings were concerned, tomorrow would be soon enough for Kade to see his brothers. The following day, he'd see his two sisters, Skye and Ainsley.

He rubbed his chest, knowing the hurt his siblings had experienced the past two years, believing he was dead, would be difficult to overcome. Learning the true nature of Kade's career would also come as a surprise to his brothers and sisters. For them to understand why he was reported dead, they'd need to know the whole story, and that meant telling them about K19 Security Solutions.

The four founding partners, including himself, were former agents who'd worked for the CIA's Special Activities Division of the agency's National Clandestine Service, or NCS. Three years ago, they'd collectively left government employment and founded the private security and intelligence firm. Ironically, almost one hundred percent of their assignments came from the NCS. However, they made a lot more money carrying them out than they did before.

"Welcome back, Doc," Mercer said, embracing him before he walked Quinn out to the transport vehicle waiting to take them to the safe house in Harmony.

"Good to be back."

"How's Leech?" Mercer asked.

"We flew him to Ramstein. He should be cleared for travel in a few days."

"Anything I can do?"

"Paps and Razor are still over there. Let's get 'em out as soon as we can."

"They're already out, sir. Someone named Fatale arranged transport."

Merrigan Shaw, or Fatale as Mercer had referred to her, was an MI6 agent who'd briefed him on Calder's return to the United States.

Once Mercer was gone, Kade surveyed the building one last time.

"Moving out, sir," Dutch reported.

"I'll ride along." Kade intended to transport the two dead bodies to Camp Roberts personally.

He and Leech had taken out the rest of the Maskhadov faction when they'd mounted their escape after two years of captivity.

To Kade's knowledge, Calder had been the only surviving member of the organization responsible for killing countless US agents and operatives. The only reason he'd remained alive until today was because he'd returned to the States shortly after the Maskhadovs captured Leech.

In order to leave the country and exact his revenge, Kade had been forced to make a deal with the most unlikely allies—United Russia, the only organization who wanted the Maskhadovs dead more than the CIA did. As part of the deal, Kade had agreed to turn Calder over to UR, dead or alive.

He had no intention of leaving Calder's body until he was absolutely certain it was in UR's possession. Only then would he know that the nightmare that began over twenty years ago was finally over.

2

Kade

Hours later, the hand off of Calder's body happened quickly and covertly, which meant he was free to meet the others in Harmony.

"Quinn's asleep," Mercer told Kade when he walked in the door that led from the garage into the house.

"Where's Ma?" he asked right as she came around the corner, almost knocking him over.

She held him tight as her body shook with cries of happiness, and she murmured what Kade could only assume was a prayer of thankfulness. At the same time, his father rested his hand on his shoulder.

Out of the corner of his eye, he saw Quinn come around the same way his mother had. Her bewildered gaze traveled back and forth between him and Mercer.

"How are you feeling?" Kade asked after his mother released him.

"Okay," she murmured.

"Would you like to talk?"

"Now?" she asked, once again looking at Mercer.

"It doesn't have to be," said Kade. "But we can if you want to. I'm sure you have questions."

It was only when Mercer reached his hand out to her that Quinn came all the way into the room.

"There isn't any rush, precious," Kade heard him say to her.

"My head hurts." She turned to Sorcha, who rushed to the sink to get Quinn a glass of water.

"Drink this, precious," she said, which made both Quinn and Mercer smile. "And take these," she added, handing her what looked like aspirin.

"How about you, Da?" Kade asked, wondering if they should consider taking him and Quinn to the hospital.

Before his father could answer, his mother pointed to a bag sitting on the table. "Have someone run this to the hospital and ask Susan in the lab to analyze it."

Of course his father had made sure to collect the cloth used to knock him out, or maybe it had been the one used on Quinn. Regardless, having tests run to determine whether simple ether or something more powerful had been used should be done immediately.

Kade wished they'd let him know earlier; he would've taken it to Camp Roberts with him. He looked over at Mercer, who was studying something on his phone.

"What's up?" Kade asked.

"It was chloroform. Someone beat you to it," he reported.

"Who?"

"Dutch. Apparently, he picked up a second cloth at the scene."

"Who uses chloroform these days?" said his mother.

It was a valid question, although, with the Russians, it depended more on what they could get their hands on.

"Whose orders did Dutch act on?" Kade snapped at no one in particular.

"Mine," said his father.

"Sorry, Da." Kade rolled his shoulders. He needed to decompress—something he'd always made arrangements to do in the past before he came home. This time, his return was like no other. He'd been gone over two years. First, he'd been deep undercover, and then the majority of it he'd been held in captivity. Not to mention, reported dead.

"I need a minute." Kade walked out the back door.

Mercer came out later and offered him a beer. "Want one?"

"Six pack would be better."

Kade twisted the cap off and downed half the bottle. "Been a damn long time."

"Do what you need to do, Doc."

"Yeah?"

"Yeah. Everyone is going to understand, and if they don't, screw 'em."

"Even if what I need to do is escape to a deserted island somewhere?"

Mercer laughed and nodded.

As tempting as it was, this time, for the first time, Kade had to put his family before himself, something he'd never been able to do before. Quinn needed him now, if only to explain the last twenty-one years of her life.

He leaned forward and rested his forearms on his knees. "I don't know where to start," he said. "How is she?"

"Quinn? She's okay. She has questions, but she knows more than you think she does."

Mercer told him about the time they'd spent at Casa Carrizo, the house in Montecito where she'd spent the first seven years of her life, and how Laird had also given her access to the apartment above the winery.

"She remembers me."

"She does. Bits and pieces at least. She remembers you teaching her how to ride a bike."

Kade smiled. He remembered that day well for its normalcy. He, Lena, and Quinn had spent the morning in town. When they came back to the house, he'd asked if she was ready for him to take the training wheels off her bike. She'd told him she was scared, and he'd promised her he wouldn't let go until he was sure she was ready. Quinn hadn't pedaled twenty feet before she wanted to try on her own. She'd ridden around and around the circular drive, making him dizzy. He could still hear the sound of her giggling.

Two days later, before the crack of dawn, he'd left on another mission. Lena had begged him not to go, even though she knew damn well he had no choice. The joy he'd felt with Quinn was replaced by guilt and remorse. His guilt, though, wasn't because he was sorry he had to leave. Instead, it was because he couldn't wait to get out of there.

"I'm a selfish bastard," he muttered. "Always have been." He looked up at Mercer. "Right now, all I want to do is leave. That's about as honest as I've ever been, Eighty-eight."

Mercer took a swig of his beer. "Talk to Quinn first, and then leave. However much time you need, take it. I know, without you saying a word, that you've been to hell and back. You look like it too."

Kade laughed. He knew it too. His body was soft, and he probably weighed fifty pounds less than he had when he left.

"I can't, not until I've seen everyone. By the way, how's Lena?"

"No different."

Kade laughed again. "She can come back now."

Mercer shook his head and looked away.

"What?"

"If it weren't for Quinn, I'd say we should let her stay gone."

Kade knew exactly what Mercer meant. "She wasn't always this bad."

"Paps told me."

"Paps? Interesting."

Mercer laughed too. "I've never seen two people hate each other more than Paps and Lena."

"You know what they say about love and hate."

"Not this time." Mercer shook his head. "So, who's Fatale?"

"MI6."

"How'd he get involved in your mission in Moscow?"

"She."

"Huh?"

"Fatale is a woman, and to answer your question, she infiltrated the Maskhadovs about six months ago."

"What was she after?"

"Same thing they were." Same thing Calder was. Same thing he was. MI6, CIA, UR—everybody was after what Calder had hidden over twenty years ago.

"Must be important, considering Calder was willing to kill me to get it," said Quinn.

He hadn't heard her come out the back door. Kade stood. "Have a seat."

"No, thanks. I just came out to see if you were hungry. Sorcha made cock-a-leekie soup."

"She did? Huh." Kade scratched his chin.

"It's my favorite."

"You used to…Well, that was a long time ago."

"No, tell me. Please." Quinn sat in one of the other empty chairs and motioned for Kade to join her.

He told her about her mother insisting she wouldn't like it, but she had, even when she was little enough to still be in a high chair.

"You used to call it—"

"Kukie-lukie." Quinn laughed. "I remember now."

"Excuse me." Mercer stood and went inside.

"I, uh, guess I better get used to this. There's a lot I need to tell you, not just stories about soup, but about your life, Quinn."

"Not today," she murmured, her eyes filling with tears.

"You asked me a question—"

She stood. "Don't answer. Not yet."

"Where the hell is everybody?" Kade said to himself the next morning. He remembered sitting in the recliner after dinner, and not much after that. At some point, he must've gone into the bedroom since that's where he was when he woke up.

He found coffee in a cupboard, brewed a pot, and went out the door to the deck. He sat in the chair Quinn was in the night before, and contemplated her reaction to him. She'd directly asked if he was her father, and when he'd tried to answer, she refused to let him.

He shook his head. He shouldn't have been surprised; she was a lot like her mother. She looked like her too. Before Calder almost killed her, Lena's eyes lit up the same way Quinn's did.

He'd never seen anyone with eyes like hers—deep mahogany pools as rich as the vineyard's soil, with lightning strikes of cinnamon. Her porcelain skin was like his mother's, but instead of fiery red like hers, Lena's hair was golden blonde.

Her code name was Barbie, and Kade still remembered the night she'd been given it.

***

"I still haven't figured out what to call you," Kade heard Calder murmur when she walked past him.

"Lena works fine for me."

"What's the actress' name…Lena Horny?" he whispered, but Kade could still hear him.

"Very funny. It's pronounced 'horn.'" Kade snapped.

"I like the other way better," he added before walking away.

Kade watched the way Lena's cheeks flushed, and wanted to slam his fist in Calder's face for humiliating her. He acknowledged the overreaction. It happened often with his fellow recruit, and it troubled him.

He excused himself from the conversation he hadn't been listening to between his father and hers.

"Lena, right?" he asked. "You went to Paso Robles High. Were you a year or two years behind me?"

"Just a year," she answered. "I didn't think you'd noticed."

"Of course I noticed the prettiest girl in the building."

"Come on, Barbie," her father said, "Let's get some meat on those bones."

Lena cringed.

"Barbie?" Calder smirked, making Kade's hand ball into a fist.

"Have you ever seen those damn dolls? Tall and skinny, just like this one."

"It's my fault," Lena's mother said once they were seated at the table. "When I was packing away the toys she had as a little girl, I pulled the doll out and commented that it had long, thin arms and legs, and a tiny waist like Lena." Her mom turned to her. "I'm sorry, sweetheart. Your dad picked up on the name and hasn't let you hear the end of it since."

"Blonde hair, too," her father added.

"Thanks, Dad," she murmured, refusing to look anywhere but at her plate.

Kade didn't know a damn thing about dolls, but if Lena looked like this "Barbie," it had to be beautiful. He wished she would smile. When she did, her rose-colored lips curved so perfectly that they looked drawn on.

He didn't realize he was staring, until her eyes met his and her cheeks turned the same rose color as her lips. He let his gaze linger momentarily, hoping she knew that, no matter how embarrassed she might be by her father's teasing, there was at least one man who found her breathtaking.

When he looked away, his eyes met her father's. Leech hadn't missed any of what passed between Kade and his daughter, and while he expected to see anger, instead, he saw approval.

"Break her heart, and I'll break your neck," Leech murmured later when they were helping clear the dishes from the table.

"What's this?" Calder asked.

"Never you mind," Kade answered.

***

From that day on, her code name had been Barbie, although Kade had never referred to her by it. He knew how much she hated it.

His cell pinged with a motion alert from the app his father had installed on his phone the night before. He swiped his finger across the screen and saw Paps, Razor, and someone he didn't expect to be with them: Merrigan "Fatale" Shaw.

3

Merrigan

This was a terrible idea. Her instincts had told her so when Paps suggested she fly back to the States with them. When she'd argued, he insisted, telling her it was her boss who had made the suggestion.

"Our mission isn't over," Paps reminded her this morning as they drove to the house where Kade was staying. "United Russia won't stop looking for whatever they believe Calder had on them. While they'll honor the agreement they made with Doc, since they have no reason to believe Barbie or Skipper were involved, I guarantee they're setting up shop here in California as we speak."

"Barbie and Skipper?"

"Doc's wife and daughter."

He was married? The last time she saw Doc Butler, the kiss they'd shared made her knees weak and every other part of her body react like he was her own personal sexual beacon. And now, to find out the bastard was married? She was as angry as she was disappointed.

She was also ready to return to the UK on the first flight she could book.

The more she thought about it, though, the more she decided his being married was actually a blessing. An affair between a former high-ranking CIA agent and an MI6 agent of equal standing was beyond unprofessional.

When they arrived at the house, Merrigan stood on the porch and watched the reunion between Kade, Paps, and Razor, getting emotional, knowing how she'd feel, seeing a colleague who had been long-thought dead.

She stole glances at Kade as he spoke to his team-mates. Even after being tortured and malnourished for several months, his arms remained so muscular they looked like boulders, and nothing could diminish the breadth of his shoulders. Kade had a swagger that exuded the confidence of a man who knew he was the best in the business, regardless of the fact that he'd been held captive and tortured for months. His eyes were so blue they looked like ocean water, and he sported a warm smile she'd rarely seen. Doc Butler could easily make any woman drop her panties. Merrigan included.

"Fatale," Kade said, nodding his head.

"Doc," she responded.

"Come on in." He motioned to the door Paps and Razor were walking through.

She went inside, looking around for his damned wife. It wasn't fair of Merrigan to damn the woman; it wasn't her fault her husband was a bloody womanizer.

"What are you looking for?" he asked, sauntering over to her.

"Nothing," she answered with a clip that reminded her of her mother's voice when she was angry.

He smiled. "How are you, Fatale?"

"I'm fine. Thanks."

"What are you doing here?"

"She's here on behalf of MI6, Doc," Paps answered for her.

"As a matter of fact, I was just leaving."

"Where to?"

She shot a glare in his direction, still incredulous he'd never thought to mention a wife or daughter in the time she'd known him.

"I asked where you're staying."

"I'm not certain yet." She turned to Paps. "I'll get in touch later."

She pretended not to notice Kade had followed her out the front door, and was in the car, with the door almost closed, when he caught up with her.

"Merrigan?"

"We'll speak later, Doc."

"Kade."

She turned and looked at him for the first time since walking out of the house. "What?"

"My name is Kade."

She turned her head away, unable to look at him a moment longer.

"The last time we saw each other—"

"Seriously? You're bringing that up now? And here of all places."

"What does where we are have to do with anything?"

"I've got to go."

"You could stay here," he said before she could close the door.

"You're *unreal*." She wrenched the handle, slammed it shut, and backed out of the driveway.

4

Kade

Kade stalked back to the house. Merrigan was behaving like a teenager embarrassed by their kiss instead of the badass take-no-prisoners agent she'd been in Moscow.

"What the hell was that about?" he asked Paps when he came back inside.

"No idea."

"Why is she here?"

"Because the mission isn't over, Doc," Razor chimed in.

"Right." Kade was aware of that much, but now that Quinn and her mother were out of danger, and he and Leech had personally witnessed the demise of the Maskhadov organization, he didn't feel the same sense of urgency to put himself or his team on the line to find something that impacted United Russia more than himself, his family, or his country.

"How much do you know about Eighty-eight and Skipper?" Paps asked.

"Everything I need to." The nature of their relationship was obvious. Whatever he hadn't picked up on when he killed Calder, he'd learned yesterday.

"Incoming," Razor said, looking out the front window.

For a split second, Kade hoped that meant Merrigan was back, until he saw his brother Maddox climbing out of an SUV parked in the driveway. He waited to see if anyone was with him, and was relieved when no one else exited the vehicle. He could handle one brother at a time better than all three at once.

Kade took a deep breath and opened the door, waiting for his brother to notice him. When their eyes locked, he met Maddox halfway.

"Thank fucking God. When Da told me you were alive, I prayed I wasn't dreaming." Maddox's eyes filled with tears when they were close enough to embrace.

"How are you, Mad?" Kade asked, not knowing what else to say.

"Hell of a lot better after seeing you in the flesh."

Their embrace went on and on, neither of them wanting to let go. While his reunion with Paps and Razor had been emotional, it was nothing compared to seeing his brother again. It would be the same with the rest of his siblings.

"Come inside," Kade said a few minutes later. "Let's talk."

"What a way to celebrate New Year's Day. I think this is going to be a great one," Maddox said, smiling through his tears.

"Damn. The date went right by me." Kade squeezed Mad's shoulder. "It's so good to see you, my brother."

"You have no idea how often I've dreamed of this. Naught and Brodie don't know you're back yet," Maddox told him. "Like I said, Da thought it was better I knew what I was walking into."

"I want to see them as soon as possible."

"How about now? Naught's at Butler Ranch. I'm not sure about Brodie."

"Let's go." Kade turned to look at Paps and Razor, who waved him off.

On the drive, Kade filled Maddox in on everything he could about the last two years of his life, and about his marriage to Lena and their daughter. Then he told him about the K19 team and how he'd asked them to look after his family.

"They were with you in Argentina," Kade said. "Although at the time, I knew nothing about what was going on here."

"Tell me what you do know," said Maddox.

"Eighty-eight—one of my partners—and Da briefed me yesterday." Kade couldn't believe all three of his brothers were married, that Brodie and Peyton were new parents of a baby girl, and that Alex was pregnant.

Ainsley was the only one of his siblings not married, but Ma had told him she and Cristobal Avila had gotten engaged on Christmas. She'd also told him about Brodie and Peyton's relationship and that his youngest brother had been thought dead after the plane he was on crashed in the Argentinian mountains.

What he hadn't told his mother, because it would sound like he had gone batshit crazy, was that so much of what she told him, he felt as though he already knew. Maybe not the specific details, but enough that he'd had a sense of déjà vu.

Maddox sent Naughton a message, saying he was on his way to Butler Ranch and needed to meet with him. In typical Naught fashion, he gave Mad a ration of shit about not telling him why.

"Da made it easier on me," Maddox told him. "I'm not sure how I would've reacted if you'd showed up without warning."

Kade understood, but Naughton was different. Knowing in advance wouldn't be better for him.

"Maybe I should go in first," Mad suggested.

"No. I'll handle it."

When they pulled through the gates of the ranch where he'd grown up, a sense of peace washed over him. He'd made the decision not to come here last night because he wasn't ready to see his brothers, but now that he was here, he knew he wouldn't spend another night in Harmony.

Maybe if he weren't there, Merrigan would consider staying at the house rather than at a hotel. Although she might feel uncomfortable with Paps and Razor. He should've thought of that earlier.

Could that be what was behind her strange behavior? He couldn't think about her right now, though; he was about to see his brother for the first time in two years.

He knocked, and the door flew open.

"What the hell—" Naughton began, but stopped talking when he saw Kade standing in front of him.

Like with Maddox, the embrace they shared lingered.

"I knew you were alive," Naughton muttered. "I prayed I wasn't wrong."

Unlike Maddox, he didn't want to know where Kade had been or why he was reported dead. All he cared about was that his brother was home. "You can tell me some other time. Right now, there's someone I want you to meet."

Kade and Maddox followed Naught inside and waited in the living room while he went to get his wife.

"This is Bradley," he said when they came downstairs. "And, sweetheart, this is my brother Kade."

Bradley's eyes filled with tears, and instead of shaking his outstretched hand, she hugged him. "It's so nice to meet you," she murmured.

Before she let go, the front door flew open.

"*Oh my God,*" screamed Alex, running over to him. "Tell me you're real. Tell me I'm not dreaming. I have dreamed about you, just so you know. And I'm getting damn tired of the lectures you give me when I do. God, I'm glad to see you." She pulled back and looked him up and down. "You look like shit, by the way, but I guess being dead will do that to a guy." She took a deep breath. "Wow, what a way to celebrate the new year."

Alex held him so tight that Kade could feel every stuttered breath she took as she rested her cheek on his chest and cried.

"How'd you know, Al?" Maddox asked her.

"Sorcha told me there was someone visiting Naughton who I'd want to see. I was halfway here by the time she finished her sentence. I *knew*. Don't ask me how, but I knew."

Kade had wondered countless times while being held by the Russians if the connection between him and his family was strong enough that they'd know he wasn't dead. He'd wondered the same thing with his K19 partners, although with them, the agreement had been to accept the report and act accordingly, but not to put a marker on any grave until they saw one another's dead bodies with their own eyes. That's how he'd known they'd never stop looking for him.

"When are you going to see Peyton and Brodie?" she asked and then continued without giving him a chance to respond. "You know they're married and have a baby, right?" Alex patted her stomach and then pulled Kade's hand to rest on it. "I'm pregnant. Did Mad tell you? I'm due in July."

Kade smiled. He'd always loved Alex and had banked on Maddox figuring out he couldn't live without her. By the look on his brother's face, he had.

"They named the baby Kismet Kadence, for you, in part. Oh, and Skye and Mac named their boy Kade. Did you know?" She walked over and put her arms around Mad's waist. "Thanks for the house, and the vineyards, and everything else you gave us, by the way."

"You're welcome," he said and looked over at Naughton and his wife.

"Now that you're back..." Naughton began, but Kade stopped him.

"Nothing changes."

"But—"

"Nothing. It's all yours." He looked back and forth between his brothers. "Both of yours."

"So Peyton..." said Alex.

Kade wasn't worried about Peyton. He'd spent a lot of time thinking about her when the Russians left him alone long enough for his mind to process anything beyond the daily pain they'd inflicted on his body.

She'd known, even before he left to rescue Leech, that they weren't meant to be. He adored her and her boys, and had even tried to convince himself that he wanted to marry her. As soon as he'd told his family so, he knew it was wrong. It was as though saying the words out loud was enough to convince him it didn't feel right. He was happy to hear she and Brodie were together; it was what he'd wanted.

"They thought Brodie was dead too," he heard Alex say. "Jamie and Finn will be fine, I think, don't you?"

Kade realized she'd addressed her question to him, and he didn't know how to answer. They were the two people whose reaction he was most concerned about. He loved Peyton's boys and hoped they'd eventually accept him as their uncle.

"Did anyone else see him?" he heard Alex ask Mad.

"I'm not sure. Why?"

"You know how fast news spreads in this valley. I'd hate for Brodie and Peyton to hear Kade was back via gossip."

She was right. Kade wouldn't want that, either. "Do you know where they are?" he asked.

"Home," answered Naught. "Wait until you see their house."

After another emotional reunion with Brodie, Kade sat on the front porch, talking to Peyton. He explained as much as he could about his ordeal, and she told him about falling in love with his brother and thanked him for bringing them together.

"I have a question, but not about anything important. It's more something I'm curious about."

"You can ask me anything."

Peyton smiled. "But that doesn't mean you'll be able to answer."

Kade smiled too. "You know the drill."

"The night before you were reported *missing,* you sent me a photo. I could've sworn it looked like Bagram in Afghanistan."

"Good eye. And yeah, I stopped there for an intelligence briefing."

Peyton nodded. "Like I said, I was curious." She stood to go inside. "I want you to know I do love you, Kade."

"And I love you. I always will."

She stood on tiptoes and kissed his cheek, then smiled. "You're my brother now."

"And the boys' uncle. How do you think they'll react?"

"They'll be fine. Trust me. Kids are so resilient."

"Ma has a family dinner planned tonight. She's invited Skye and Ainsley as well, given New Year's Day dinner is a family tradition," Brodie told Kade when he and Peyton came in the house.

He wanted more time with all of his siblings, and the dinner Ma had planned would give him the opportunity. Within a few days, he hoped the relationships he had with them would return to the way they were before he left for Moscow.

Once everyone knew of his return, and he got Leech and maybe even Lena settled, he'd spend more time with Quinn before he decided what to do with the rest of his life. The only thing he knew for certain was he wouldn't be returning to the spy game. Never if he could help it. There were other ways he could serve his country.

When Maddox dropped him off at the house in Harmony, Da's old truck was in the driveway, but when he went inside, his father wasn't there, although Paps and Razor were.

"Hey, Doc," said Razor. "These are for you." He tossed Kade a set of keys.

"Did you locate Merrigan?"

Paps nodded. "Moonstone Cottages. Number four. It's in the front. I've scheduled a meeting for nineteen hundred hours," Paps told him. "Oh, and Barbie will be back in the morning."

"Roger that," he answered. "But push the meeting to tomorrow."

He walked out, shutting the front door behind him. As soon as he set things straight with Merrigan, he planned to meet up with Quinn and Mercer.

Naught had told him they were invited to tonight's dinner, but he hoped to have some time alone with the two of them before that to help prepare her for what to expect. He checked the time, realizing he might not be able to fit it in unless things resolved easily with Merrigan, and that, he doubted.

5

Merrigan

Merrigan checked into one of several bed-and-breakfast places scattered along Moonstone Beach Road in Cambria. Kade had talked about it so often when the Russians would leave them alone that she felt as though she'd been here before, and was stunned to find it looked exactly the way she'd imagined it.

She wouldn't be staying here long, though. In a few hours, she had a call scheduled with her superior, during which she intended to ask for a replacement. If she had to, she'd admit the relationship between her and Doc had become personal. It might mean she'd be asked to leave MI6, but that, she could handle. Seeing Kade with his wife was more than she could bear.

Meeting at 1900 hours, said the text from Paps.

Where? she answered.

When Paps told her they'd meet at the house where she'd dropped them off, she bristled and asked for an alternate location. She was still waiting for a response when a text came in from Kade.

We need to talk, it said.

Merrigan started and stopped several different messages in reply, but ultimately, didn't respond. Ten minutes later, her cell rang.

"Fatale," she answered, even though the caller ID told her Kade was calling.

"I know you received my message, so quit playing games. We need to talk."

"You should know I've requested a new assignment."

"Good."

Good? What the hell? Evidently, he wanted her gone as much as she wanted to be.

"Then, we have nothing to talk about."

"Sure we do. Where are you? Moonstone?"

"No."

"Don't lie to me."

God, this man infuriated her. She should just hang up on him, but she couldn't bring herself to disconnect the call. If this was going to be the last time she heard the voice she'd grown to crave, a few minutes more wouldn't make a difference.

"You know I'll find you whether you tell me where you are or not."

"I'm leaving for Los Angeles shortly; I'm returning to London."

"You're lying to me again, and I want to know why."

"Kade, please. We both know how inappropriate this conversation is. What happened in Moscow shouldn't have. I've made Rivet aware of the situation, and he—"

"Stop this. I know you haven't made Rivet aware of a damn thing. I'll see you in an hour."

Her phone beeped, indicating the end of that conversation. Instead of setting the phone down, she made the call she'd told Kade she already had.

"Fatale," said Rivet on the other end of the line.

"Sir."

"The answer is no."

"What is the question?"

"I'm not reassigning you, nor am I sending in a replacement."

Rivet could be so bloody annoying. "Why ever not?"

"Stay the course. You've come this far. See it through."

"But—"

"I don't give a toss what's happened with you and Butler. You're both adults."

The call ended the same way her call with Kade had.

She rolled her shoulders. A transfer may not happen straight away, but that didn't mean she and Kade would be anything but fellow operatives assigned to the same mission. Her will to be professional would simply have to overcome her will to feel his naked body against hers.

When she heard the knock on the door, Merrigan knew Kade stood on the opposite side of it. She squared her shoulders and yanked it open, ready to give him a piece of her mind.

He crossed the threshold and lifted her in his arms before she was able to say as much as hello. His mouth came down on hers hard, as his tongue demanded entry.

This is what she'd fantasized about since they parted ways in Moscow, after the scorching kiss they'd shared.

When he carried her over to the bed and was about to trap her body under his, Merrigan came to her senses and rolled out from under him.

"What in the hell do you think you're doing?" She wiped his taste from her lips with the back of her hand.

Kade stalked toward her, forcing her into a corner. "Picking up where we left off," he murmured, then kissed her again.

"Stop this," she said, pushing against him.

Instead of letting her go, Kade barricaded her between the wall and his body. He dipped his head until he found his target and pressed his lips against hers. It wasn't just her lips he kissed, either. His tongue trailed down her neck, and his hand sneaked under her sweater.

It was as though her body had a mind of its own and refused to listen to her brain telling it to get away from him, especially when he took her nipple into his mouth.

Finally, she found the single word she knew would bring this seduction to a screeching halt.

"Barbie," she murmured when he took a breath.

"She won't be here until tomorrow."

Merrigan pushed at Kade with all her might, catching him off guard long enough to slip under his arm. *"You bastard,"* she screeched at him. *"How dare you?"*

Kade held up his hands but stalked toward her. She didn't have much space to get away from him in the small room, but if she could maneuver herself closer to the door, maybe she could run out, get in her car, and leave before he realized what was happening.

Unfortunately, he was quicker than her. He scooped her up and set her on the edge of the bed, pinning her with his body.

"Explain," he bellowed. "Right now."

"I'm not sure what kind of women you're used to, Doc, but I am not one of them."

"Are you telling me you don't want this?"

His lips were close enough that he could easily kiss her again, and if he did, she doubted she'd be able to maintain her resolve.

"That's exactly what I'm telling you," she said, refusing to look at him.

His grip loosened but not enough that she could slip away from him again. "What does this have to do with *Barbie?*"

"Oh. My. God," she roared. "It has everything to do with her. Kade, have you no respect for her, or me, or

any other woman? How could I have misjudged you so completely?"

He let go and stood, walking over to the table by the window. He pulled out one of the chairs and turned it so he was facing her. "Let's start over. How do you know who Barbie is?"

"How I know is unimportant."

"Tell me."

"Don't be daft. I'm in no mood for games."

"Neither am I. Now, tell me who you think Barbie is."

"For Christ's sake. She's your bloody wife."

His face softened, and Merrigan thought maybe she'd even seen a smile. "She's my bloody *ex*-wife. We've been divorced for almost fifteen years."

"But…"

Kade raised a brow and waited for her to continue. When she didn't, he spoke. "Where did you get the idea she was still my wife?"

She thought hard about Paps' words earlier. Had she somehow misheard him? Had he said ex-wife, but instead, she'd heard wife? "I must've misunderstood," she said, raising her chin.

When she stood, so did he.

"Come here," he said, even though she was close enough that he could've easily pulled her into his arms.

She hesitated, feeling foolish for letting him see how much thinking he was married had affected her. They'd shared one kiss before today. Just one. It didn't matter that it had curled her toes and set her body aflame. One kiss, no matter how incendiary, did not give her license to be jealous.

His gaze rested on her still unopened suitcase, and instead of moving closer to her, he picked it up and turned in the direction of the door.

"Where do you think you're going with that?"

"There's somewhere I want to take you."

"If it requires a different attire, I can change here. We don't need my entire trunk."

"I'm taking you to my family's ranch. You can stay there."

She folded her arms. "I'm perfectly comfortable here."

Kade looked around the small room and shook his head. "I'm not." He walked out the door, carrying her bag with him. "Let's go," he said behind him.

"Kade, I—"

He dropped her trunk where he stood and stalked back over to her, grasping her neck with one hand and her waist with the other as his lips came crashing down on hers. His tongue wound its way through her parted lips, and his fingers dug into the flesh of her hip. She whimpered when he pressed his body to hers and she felt his hardness.

He pulled back enough to look into her eyes, but his body remained flush with hers.

"I haven't seen my family for two years. Most of them believed I was dead. I've seen my daughter, actually held her, looked into her eyes, and spoken to her for the first time in fourteen years, and yet, you are all I can think about. My mother is hosting a family dinner tonight, and if I have any hope of being present with the people who mean more to me than anything else in this world, I need you by my side. Do you understand, Merrigan? Don't make me beg you to come with me. Come with me because you want to."

She took a deep breath and studied him. "Okay."

He sighed. "Thank you."

He let her go and put her bag in the bed of an old truck, then opened the passenger door for her. "What about my car?" she asked, looking at the vehicle parked next to his.

"Someone will bring it to the ranch."

"Wouldn't it be easier if I followed you?"

Kade motioned for her to get in, and when she did, he leaned in so his lips were almost touching hers. "No."

Merrigan laughed when he backed away and closed her door. How could she not? All that drama for one simple word.

6

Kade

He glanced at Merrigan who, instead of looking at him, focused her attention on the Pacific Ocean as he drove her away from it.

Maybe he was being a shit by asking her to stay thirty miles inland with him, but he couldn't help it. He couldn't stand to be away from her. Even between the time he left Moscow and when she arrived with Paps and Razor, he'd missed her. When she'd shown up unexpectedly, half of him wondered why she was there, while the other half thanked God she was close enough to touch.

It had been so long since he'd allowed himself to *feel*. Every day he'd spent in captivity, he buried every possible emotion deeper and deeper, until he felt more machine than man.

Was that all this unyielding need for her was—his emotions bubbling to the surface faster than he could manage them? No, it had to be more than that. When he looked at Merrigan it was as though his eyes focused for the first time in his life.

Colors were brighter. He felt the wind's light touch on every part of his exposed skin, and the sound of her laugh was like a chorus of angels. This shit was so not him. A chorus of angels? *Fuck.*

What he really felt was alive and free—free to finally touch the beautiful woman sitting beside him. Her red hair was darker than his ma's and had both brown and blonde woven through the wavy tendrils that flowed down past her shoulders. Her skin was pale, yet had a natural rosy glow, and her blue eyes sparkled as though they were sapphires cut with diamonds.

Finally, today, he'd felt the bare skin of her breasts beneath his hands, and he longed for so much more.

The first time he'd seen Merrigan he was in the hell hole where the Russians kept Leech and him barely alive, yet lucid enough that they believed the next beating would force the answers they sought out of them. Initially, he'd thought she was an angel and that his time had finally come.

When he heard her speak to the men in Russian, he thought he was hallucinating. No one that beautiful, with a purity that seemed to seep from her skin, could possibly be part of the group who beat him to a bloody pulp day in, day out.

It took three weeks of watching her come and go, waiting for some sign that she wasn't another demon, for him to know he hadn't been wrong about her. The day she finally spoke to him, with a soft Scottish lilt that reminded him of his mother, he asked her if he was dead.

"You're not dead, Doc," she whispered. "And I'm here to make sure you stay that way until I get you and Leech out of here."

Merrigan took a deep breath and let her head fall back against the seat. Her eyes drifted to him, and the slightest of smiles came over her face.

"What are you thinking?" he asked.

"We're here. It's like a dream, isn't it? After months of hearing about the beauty of this place, I'm here, and it's everything you said it would be. It's more, really."

Kade didn't answer. He couldn't. It felt as though his heart would beat out of his chest. When she reached out with her china-delicate hand and rested it on his, he felt that same purity flow from her skin to his. How could someone who had seen and done the same horrific things he had, still remain as radiant and otherworldly as Merrigan? Did God somehow cleanse her soul, keeping it free from the darkness that seemed to enshroud him? Was it insane to think that if she wrapped her goodness and light around him, he too could be cleansed from evil?

"Thank you," she murmured.

"You're welcome," he managed to say, almost afraid of the sound of his own voice.

"Do you know what I'm thanking you for?"

He laughed. "I was wondering if you could read my thoughts." Kade turned to look in her eyes. "I was just thinking you are the most beautiful woman I've ever known."

Her cheeks turned a bright rosy color, and she looked away from him.

"Thank you again, then," she murmured.

"What were you thanking me for the first time?"

"Making this real."

"I'm not sure you'll feel that way after you see how 'real' my family can be."

She turned in the seat so her body was almost facing his. "Tell me what to expect. Brief me on the Butler clan."

7

Merrigan

No amount of forewarning could've prepared Merrigan for Kade's family, even if she'd read a two-hundred-page dossier.

His mother, Sorcha, was like a gale-force wind enveloping those around her in a blanket of spun sugar. His father, Burns Butler—although no one in the family knew him that way other than Kade and Sorcha—was a legend of a man. The stories she'd heard about him, while almost mythical, didn't come close to doing him justice. It was clear his oldest son admired him both as a role model, but also as a loving father.

Maddox, who was married to Alex, smiled through dancing eyes. The two together exuded a mischievousness that was as warm as a log fire on a cold day on the Scottish moor.

While Naughton's facial features weren't distinctly the same as Kade's, their temperament was like looking at two halves of what had once been one soul.

A very beautiful woman, holding an equally cherubic baby, approached her with two young boys in tow. She'd seen Kade with them and his brother Brodie earlier. The reunion between them and their now-uncle had been both joy- and tearful.

"I'm Peyton," she said, introducing herself. "I'm Brodie's wife. And this is Kismet, our daughter, and our two boys, Jamison and Finn."

Ah. This was Peyton. Merrigan knew she was far more than Brodie's wife; she'd once been Kade's lover. "It's a pleasure to meet you. Kade has told me so much about all of you."

The boys shook her hand politely before racing off in search of something to eat. When Peyton's cheeks flushed, Merrigan took her free hand in both of hers and smiled. The look on the woman's face immediately changed, as she must've realized Merrigan and Kade were more than colleagues.

"It's a pleasure to meet you as well," Peyton said. "I hope we'll see more of you here at the ranch."

"I think you will."

Merrigan scanned the room and met Kade's lingering gaze from several paces away. He walked in her direction, his eyes never leaving hers. Did he know what his smoldering smile did to her? That every part of her warmed when he was near? Could he possibly be aware that all he'd have to do was snap his fingers, and she'd follow him to the ends of the earth?

"How are you holding up?" he asked.

"Quite well. Your family is lovely. Not at all the intimidating bunch you alluded to."

"They aren't all here yet."

"Your sisters," Merrigan murmured, remembering he had two, but not their names.

Skye arrived first, along with her husband, who Kade introduced as Mac, and two children as beautiful as Peyton's Kismet.

"This is Spencer," Kade said, hoisting the little girl up in his arms. "Spencer, this is Merrigan."

She held her hand out to the little girl, who shrunk back into her uncle's arms.

"She's shy," said Skye. "Although she doesn't seem to have any issues with Uncle Kade."

"That's Kade," said Spencer, motioning to her baby brother. "You're not Kade." She put her palm on his face. "Tell me your real name."

"Well, it is Kade, just like your baby brother. But some people call me Doc."

"Hmm. Okay, Uncle Doc. Is Merry your wife?"

"No, sweet girl, I'm his friend."

"You sound like G'ma Sorcha." Spencer wriggled free from Kade and slid to the ground, taking Merrigan's hand and leading her to her grandmother.

"Grandma, I think Merry is a Scot."

"Aye, lass. I believe you're right, but her name is Merrigan. Try again, Spencer. Say 'Merr-i-gan.'"

"But I like Merry."

"I do too," said Kade, putting his hand on Merrigan's waist. "Very much," he whispered.

"I think Uncle Doc should marry Merry," said Spencer, bursting into a fit of giggles. "Marry, Merry, marry, Merry." She twirled around the room, singing.

"How's that for real?" he said.

"She's precious."

"*Mo thruaigh mise,*" cried Sorcha. "*Càite bheil Quinn?*"

"She and Eighty…uh…Mercer are on their way."

His mother clapped her hands as she went to take baby Kade out of Skye's arms.

"I didn't realize you spoke Gaelic," Merrigan said.

"I don't, and neither does she. Not really. Every once in a while, a few words and phrases slip out, usually without her realizing it. My brothers and I pay more attention to her tone than the words she's speaking."

"So, Quinn…" Kade had told Merrigan a little about her on the drive. She'd sensed hesitancy and hadn't pushed when he didn't elaborate.

"I'm afraid she's going to be more overwhelmed than you are."

"Maybe so, but your family is very welcoming."

"She'll be…"

"What? Finish your thought."

"I was going to say she'll be under more scrutiny than you are, but I don't believe that's possible."

The front door opened, and a whirling dervish Merrigan could only guess was Ainsley flew into her brother's arms.

Merrigan walked away, not wanting to intrude on their emotional reunion. When she stood off to the side, Alex approached her.

"You're good for him," she said, nudging Merrigan with her elbow. "I've known Kade my whole life, and I've never seen him look at anyone the way he looks at you. That includes Peyton."

"We're friends—"

"Right." Alex laughed. "Maddox and I used to be *friends* too."

A man walked up and kissed Alex's cheek. "Hey, baby sister. Who's this?"

"This is Merrigan Shaw, Kade's date…I mean *friend.*" She smirked. "This is my brother Cristobal. He's engaged to Ainsley."

"Oh," slipped out before she could stop herself.

"Yep, nothing like a little Paso Robles inbreeding to make the grapes grow."

"She doesn't know what she's spouting off about," Cris said when Alex left in search of Maddox. "How are you holding up?"

"Me? Goodness, I'm fine. I feel a bit like an interloper, however."

"Nah. The Butlers are one big happy family, and if you're here, you're an official member."

"*That* is overwhelming."

A few minutes later, Kade and his sister joined her and Cris.

"I'm sorry," she said. "I can't stop crying. I'm Ainsley." Instead of shaking hands, she pulled Merrigan into an embrace. She hugged her tight, then took a step back. "Damn, Kade. She's gorgeous. Isn't she, Cris?"

"Yes, Ains," he said, wrapping his arms around her slight waist. "But I think you may be embarrassing Merrigan."

"I'm fine," she said, noticing Kade studying his phone.

He looked up and into her eyes. "They're here," he said, squeezing her hand.

Merrigan was surprised to see Paps and Razor walk in behind the people she guessed were Quinn and Mercer, but they were a welcome sight amongst all the Butlers. It wasn't as though they weren't very nice, and exceedingly welcoming, but Kade had been right; the scrutiny was intense.

Now, though, all eyes were on Quinn, and she looked as though she felt the weight of every one of them. Kade approached, tentative at first, but quickly swept her into a hug, which seemed to calm her. All the while, Mercer kept his hand first on her shoulder, then when she backed away from Kade, he rested it on the small of her back.

Like Merrigan, Mercer's eyes scanned the room, taking in every reaction, poised to act if needed. Paps and Razor were no different. It didn't matter that they were with Kade's family; the instinct was innate.

When Kade motioned to her, Merrigan walked over to where he stood with Quinn. After introducing them, Kade and Mercer stepped away.

"Are you okay?" Merrigan asked, noticing how her hands shook.

"I have no idea," answered Quinn.

"They're very happy you're here," she murmured.

Sorcha and Ainsley were the first to join them and, soon, pulled Quinn into the midst of their family.

Kade startled Merrigan when he put his arm around her shoulders.

"I've dreamed of this day," he said, resting his head against hers. "She's finally safe."

Paps and Razor came out of the kitchen, each holding a bottle of beer. Naughton and Bradley approached with five glasses and an opened, unmarked bottle of wine.

"This is one of Bradley's vintages," Naught explained.

"I want to thank you for saving my life," Bradley said to Mercer, pouring him the first glass.

Merrigan watched Kade's teammate struggle with a response. In their line of work, once the job was done, the "bridges were burned," so all links to a particular operative were broken. It was what Laird Butler was renowned for, and where he'd gotten the code name Burns.

"You're welcome, and thanks," Mercer murmured, holding up the glass of wine and appearing so anxious to Merrigan that she was relieved when Kade clapped his hand on the man's shoulder.

"We don't do what we do for recognition," he said to his brother and Bradley. "Which is why Eighty-eight here looks so uncomfortable."

"May I?" Mercer asked, pointing to the bottle and an empty glass. "Quinn might like a taste."

"Of course," said Naughton, reaching out to shake Mercer's hand. "I don't want to put you on the spot, but I have to thank you too. If you hadn't killed Jason Calder the night he abducted Bradley, I might've lost the love of my life," he said, putting his arm around his wife's shoulders and pulling her closer to him.

"You're, uh, welcome." He poured a small amount of wine in a glass. "Be right back."

Both Merrigan and Kade watched as Mercer handed Quinn the wine but didn't interrupt her conversation with Maddox and Alex. If there were two people who could make the poor lass feel more at ease, Merrigan believed they could.

Kade pulled her close to him and kissed her temple.

"So," Razor began after Naughton and Bradley walked away. "What's up with you two?"

Kade raised a brow.

"I'm just sayin', you're the only Butler either not engaged or married."

"He's divorced. That counts," said Paps, scowling.

"What's up your ass tonight?" Razor nudged him. "Oh, wait. I know what it is. Barbie's comin' back tomorrow."

Kade shook his head. "She hates being called that. Can't you two cut her a break and call her Lena, for God's sake?"

"Got a minute?" asked Paps.

"Sure," answered Kade. "Who?"

"All of you."

Kade led them out to the front porch and closed the front door behind them.

"I have an update on Leech," Paps began.

"What's happened?" Merrigan asked, not liking the look on his face.

"His condition has taken a turn for the worse."

"Dammit," said Kade. "How bad?"

"Bad enough that *Lena* should be made aware, and instead of coming here, she should go to Ramstein."

"When's her flight?" Kade asked.

"Eleven hundred hours."

"I'll meet her, and we'll fly over together." Kade walked back in the house, leaving Merrigan outside with Paps and Razor.

"You okay?" asked Razor.

"Of course. Um, by any chance, did Doc ask either of you to bring my rental by?"

Razor raised his hand and dug in his pocket for the fob. "Here you go. It's parked behind the winery." He pointed to a building that looked more like a barn.

"Thanks, and good night, gentlemen."

"Wait," said Paps. "Where are you going?"

"Back to the beach. I've had a very long day, as I'm sure both of you have as well."

8

Kade

Kade felt sick to his stomach with worry over Leech. The man had been a part of his life since the day he stepped off the bus at boot camp almost twenty-five years ago. First, he was his commanding officer. Then his mentor. When he and Lena married, Leech became is father-in-law. Their relationship changed then. They were no longer as close as they'd been.

After the divorce, he'd expected Leech would sever all ties with him. He'd done the opposite. That was when they become friends.

"I need to talk to you," Kade said to his father. "Ma too."

Laird motioned toward the kitchen, and Kade followed his mother in.

"Leech has taken a turn."

"Oh, dear God," gasped his mother, closing her eyes with her hands clasped.

"I'll arrange for transport and meet Lena at the airfield tomorrow," he told them.

"I'll go too," said his father.

His mother opened her eyes and looked between the two men.

"What is it, Sorcha?"

"Quinn."

"What of Quinn?" his father asked.

"She should go too."

Kade nodded and went back out to the main room of the house, wondering how she'd feel about going. He saw Paps and Razor head-to-head with Mercer, but didn't see Merrigan.

Quinn was holding baby Kade on her lap and talking with Skye and Ainsley when he approached. "I'm sorry to interrupt," he began.

"What's wrong?" Ainsley asked.

"I need to talk with Quinn for a moment."

Skye took the baby and followed Ainsley to the other side of the room.

"What's wrong?" Quinn repeated Ainsley's question.

"It's your grandfather."

Her eyes filled with tears.

"He's in a hospital in Germany. My father and I will be meeting your mother at the airfield in San

Luis Obispo in the morning. I'll arrange for transport to Germany."

"Okay," she whispered.

"Would you like to go with us?"

Her eyes opened wide, and she looked beyond him. "Um, have you seen Mercer?" she asked.

Kade turned and caught the man's eye, motioning him over. "I've asked Quinn if she'd like to fly to Ramstein with us tomorrow."

Mercer nodded and took Quinn's hands in his when she reached for him. "What do you think, precious?"

"I'm not sure. My mother…" Her eyes filled with tears again, and Mercer put his arms around her.

"It's okay," he murmured.

"What if she…"

"Say it, Quinn," Mercer encouraged her.

"She might not want me there."

"May I?" Kade asked.

"Of course," answered Mercer, stepping aside.

Kade took her hands in his, the same way Mercer had, and looked into her eyes. "Listen to me. Your mother is returning here to see *you*. I know this is hard to take in, but her estrangement from you was always to protect you, not because she didn't want to be with you."

She looked over his shoulder at Mercer and then back at him.

"Okay. I'll go," she said.

Kade turned around. "What about you?"

"Your call, sir," Mercer answered.

"We'll leave for the airfield at zero nine hundred hours."

"Copy that."

Kade returned to the main room. "I'm sorry to have to tell you this tonight, but I have to return to Germany. Leech Hess is in critical condition…" He couldn't go on. He felt the same way he would if he were telling his siblings that their father or mother were dying, and that Leech meant that much to him was something they'd never understand.

"I'm going too," Laird said. "We'll leave first thing in the morning."

One by one, his brothers, sisters, and their spouses approached to say goodbye. "I'll be home in a few days," he repeated to each of them. All the while, though, his eyes scanned the room. It had been at least twenty minutes since he'd seen Merrigan.

"Excuse me for just a moment," he said to Ainsley, who waited with Cris Avila. "Where is she?" he mouthed to Razor.

"She left."

Kade turned back to his youngest sister, told her how much he loved her, and kissed her goodbye. Once she and Cris left, he stalked over to where Paps and Razor were talking with his parents.

"What do you mean 'she left'?"

"She said she had a long day and was going back to the beach."

"Goddammit," he said under his breath, hoping his mother didn't hear. "Good night, Ma." He leaned down to kiss her cheek, then turned to his father. "I'll see you at the airfield in the morning."

"Where you off to?" asked Paps.

"The beach."

On the thirty-minute drive, his mind raced with memories of Leech. He couldn't fucking die now. Not after all they'd been through together. Not after how hard they fought to stay alive.

***

Joining the Marines was something Kade had always aspired to, but it was only the first step in achieving his ultimate goal of working for the United States' Central Intelligence Agency, just like his father had before him.

The Recruit Training Depot in San Diego wasn't too far from home for him, considering other recruits were traveling from every part of the country west of the Mississippi. Yet the drive was one of the longest of his life.

The nightmares that usually only plagued him when he slept were on repeat during the five-hour bus ride.

Could he do it? When faced with things he knew nothing of, could he be brave enough to accept those challenges? Would he be able to live up to the man his father was? Or would his worst fear come true, and he'd be too much of a coward?

From the moment he stepped off the bus, he realized he'd have no time to wallow in self-doubt, and even less energy. The mental and physical challenges of Boot Camp began immediately and wouldn't offer a break longer than four hours to even sleep for thirteen weeks.

He'd noticed the man who seemed to show up at every one of Kade's exercises right after he got off the bus. He wore civilian attire, but there was no mistaking the power the man yielded. Even the sergeant major, the second highest ranking officer at the recruit depot, deferred to him. Only the brigadier general commanded more respect than this man did.

It wasn't until Family Day, the day before graduation from recruit training, that Kade learned who he was.

The man approached him as he was coming out of the Squad Bay. "Hey, Boot."

Kade, unsure how to respond to a civilian who clearly had once been a high-ranking officer, stood at modified attention. "Yes, sir?"

"At ease, son. Let's take a walk."

Kade looked in the direction of his platoon and met the eye of his drill instructor, who waved him off.

"Is your family here today, son?" the man asked.

"Yes, my parents are here, sir," Kade responded.

"We'll chat with them as well."

The man led Kade to an office in a building he'd never been in. Shortly after, his parents joined them.

"Burns, it's good to see you," the man stood and said when Kade's father walked in. "You as well, Sorcha. You're as beautiful as ever."

Kade looked back and forth between his parents and the man. The connection was obvious; this was someone his father had worked with at the agency.

The man turned to Kade. "I'm John Hess, Executive Deputy, Training and Education Command here at the base," he told him.

He went on to explain he'd served with the US Marine Corp for over thirty years and retired as a general officer in 1988.

Knowing his background made Kade all the more curious why a man with a minimum rank of brigadier general had any interest in a recruit.

"Your son has exhibited exceptional leadership skills, as well as an aptitude for, let's say, accelerated learning. You should be very proud of him," he said to Kade's parents.

Twenty minutes later, Kade knew his life would irrevocably change. Rather than heading to either the School of Infantry or Military Occupational Specialty training, he was being sent to North Carolina to complete nine months of special forces training.

"Thank you, Mr. Hess," Kade said as they were leaving.

"Call me Leech, son," he said to Kade, then turned to his father. "Again, Burns, you and Sorcha should be proud of this fine young man."

Leech told him there'd be special transport arranged for him on the day before he was scheduled to report for duty and added, "Enjoy your leave. It'll be a long time before you see another one." He shook Kade's hand and his father's before hugging his mother.

***

He couldn't lose him now, dammit. They'd spent years getting to where they were. Lena and Quinn were safe. Kade could finally get to know his daughter and Leech could witness his granddaughter's beauty—both inside and out—firsthand.

The minute the plane landed at Ramstein, Doc would do everything in his power to convince Leech that now wasn't the time to give up. They both had so fucking much to live for.

9

Merrigan

This was the life they'd all signed up for, Merrigan thought as she poured herself a shot of the Scotch she'd stopped and picked up at the liquor store on her way to the beach.

In the years since she accepted her first assignment from MI6, she'd said goodbye to more colleagues who had become dear and trusted friends than she'd like to count. There were very few she'd actually had the chance to say the words to; most had been killed in the line of duty.

She didn't know yet whether she'd return to Europe to pay her own respects to Leech. She'd decide in the morning after getting some sleep.

The sheets of the bed felt cool when she crawled between them naked. She reached over and took another swig of her Scotch, then turned off the bedside lamp. She'd left the window open so she could hear the sound of the waves crashing on the shore, hoping it would lull her to sleep. Instead, she stared into the darkness, thinking about Kade.

That he'd walked away without giving her a second thought after announcing he intended to fly to Germany the next day with his ex-wife had hurt. It hurt her as a woman, but the agent in her knew exactly how he felt, and knew she would've done the same thing. They were trained to react in the moment, to make split-second decisions, then act immediately. It was as much second nature to a man like Kade as it was to her.

So, lying in bed, fretting over his behavior was juvenile. She rolled over and hugged the pillow, wishing she'd thought to grab her bag from Kade's truck. At least then she'd have her tablet and could read until her eyes closed on their own.

Merrigan yawned and stretched, hoping the blissful peace of slumber was close. She'd just drifted off when a knock at the door jarred her awake. At first, she thought she'd dreamed it, but then it came again. It was more of a rap than a knock, as though someone was using a single knuckle as opposed to an entire fist.

She remained still, hoping whoever it was had the wrong room, until she heard Kade's voice.

"Let me in, Fatale. I'd much rather spend the night in there with you, but if I have to, I'll sleep on your doorstep."

She crawled out of bed, remembering she'd seen a terry robe on the back of the bathroom door when she was here earlier. She slipped it on and tiptoed to the door, opening it just a crack.

"What are you doing here?"

"Let me in."

She took a step back and opened the door wider, hit the switch to turn on the light, and waited for him to answer.

"Why did you leave?"

"It's late, and I was tired—"

"You couldn't have come and told me that?"

"You were otherwise…engaged."

"What does that mean? I went inside to talk to my father, and when I came back, you were gone."

She walked over and sat on the end of the bed, pulling the sash of the robe tighter and crossing her arms. "Really? Is that the way it went?"

Kade shook his head and looked over at the bottle of Scotch. "May I?"

She nodded. "Of course."

He removed the paper cover from a second glass, poured a shot, then another into the glass she'd left on the bedside table. When he handed it to her, his fingers brushed against hers, sending a chill throughout her body.

He pulled a chair over and sat in front of her, close enough that their knees touched. He downed the shot, set the glass on the floor beside him, and rested his hands on her knees. He kept his eyes glued to hers as he ran his fingers up the inside of her thighs.

"Open for me," he whispered.

Merrigan took a deep breath, powerless to do anything other than what he told her to.

"Take off the robe. Let me see you."

She set her glass on the floor near his, untied the sash, and shrugged the terry cloth off her shoulders.

"Lie back for me."

When she did, he stood above her, released the top two buttons of his shirt, and pulled it off over his head. His hands went to the buckle of his belt. He unfastened it and lowered the zipper.

"Look at me," he said when she closed her eyes.

She watched as his pants slid to the floor, and he stood before her as naked as she was.

Merrigan scooted her body closer to the headboard, as Kade lowered his over hers.

"I've wanted this since the first day I saw you," he murmured, licking from her belly button over her abdomen, until his lips reached her breasts. His hand closed on one while his mouth suckled the nipple of the other.

Her body moved against his of its own volition, her sex, drawn to his hardness.

He ran his tongue up her neck to right below her ear. "I've never wanted to be inside a woman more than I want to right now."

"Please, Kade. Don't make me wait any longer."

He shrouded himself with a condom, watching her react to him.

Finally, their bodies joined together. Merrigan didn't just feel full; she felt complete. As he moved inside of her slowly, each stroke purposeful, his eyes never left hers.

"Tell me what you're feeling."

"Everything," she said, moving beneath him when he slowed.

"Nothing, no one, has ever felt like this, Merrigan. Do you feel it too?"

As much as she wanted to tell him she knew exactly what he meant, that no one had ever made her feel the way he did, she couldn't. He was too close.

Her emotions sat on the surface, waiting to explode with love for the man who was making her feel like the most cherished woman alive. His lips and hands made love to every part of her body as he thrust into her, again and again.

"Come with me, baby," he said against her lips, and she did.

That was her first orgasm of many as they explored each other's bodies until the sun came up. There had been no time to fulfill fantasies when she was finally able to execute the extradition plan that had been months in the making. Kade had been on the soonest transport out, and thank God for that. If he hadn't arrived when he did, Calder may very well have killed both Burns and Quinn. Maybe even Mercer. She shuddered at the thought.

"That didn't feel like an aftershock," he said, looking into her eyes. "What was it?"

"My mind is racing through the events of the last few days."

"I want you to come with us to see Leech."

"Not a good idea."

"What do you mean? You've spent the last few months jeopardizing your own life to save ours. If anyone should see him now, it's you. Save his life again, Merrigan."

"Kade, I…"

"Go with me."

"You need time with your…family."

"This is about Leech. I'm not ready to let him go. Are you?"

"No, of course I'm not."

"Then, help me convince him he didn't fight for the last two years to stay alive only to give up now."

Merrigan nodded. "I'll go, but I want to take a different flight."

"Why?"

"Because I do."

"I'll give on the flight, but I want you to stay with me when we arrive."

Merrigan nodded, agreeing for now. When she arrived at Ramstein, she'd see if he still wanted her to.

10

Kade

Kade heard Quinn gasp when she saw her mother walking in their direction. "She looks so different," she mumbled.

It had been a long time since he'd seen Lena, but even to him, she looked a decade younger. She wore little or no makeup, and her hair looked more natural, with a mix of gray, blonde, and brown rather than the dyed platinum she'd worn for years. It was more than that, though. The tautness of her always stress-lined face had softened, and for the first time since before Quinn was born, the corners of her mouth turned up instead of down, even though she wasn't necessarily smiling.

Lena hadn't noticed them yet, and Kade worried what her reaction would be when she saw Quinn. He wished now that he'd sent her a message, letting her know they were meeting her.

He knew Quinn was watching as intently as he was, and if her mother showed any sign of being unhappy to see her, their daughter would be devastated to the point she might change her mind about traveling to see Leech.

There was no reason more powerful for him to fight to stay alive than finally being able to get to know his granddaughter without every day being mired in worry.

Lena's eyes met his, at first questioning, then they rested on the woman standing beside him. He held his breath like he knew Quinn was, until her mother's eyes filled with tears, and she smiled in a way he didn't remember ever seeing before.

For the first time since he left Merrigan at the bed and breakfast this morning, he appreciated her suggestion to take a different flight. This moment between Quinn, her mother, and him was sacred. Even Mercer stepped away to allow their family the space they needed to connect in a way that hadn't been possible since Quinn was seven years old.

Kade watched as his daughter slowly approached her mother, and the two women embraced like he had when he reunited with his siblings.

His own eyes filled, and he watched them smile through happy tears. When Lena extended her hand in his direction, he walked forward and joined their embrace.

"I'm so sorry," he heard Lena whisper to Quinn.

"There's nothing for you to be sorry for," Kade told her.

"But all the years—"

It was Quinn who silenced her mother's words when she said, "Mom, there is no future in our past. Let's start over today, right now, and instead of dwelling on things we can't change, let's make memories we can cherish forever."

As proud as he was of Quinn and the maturity she'd just exhibited, the question of the identity of her father still lingered over all of them. He couldn't allow her to continue to put off knowing the truth by avoiding the past.

"Why are you all here?" Lena asked, noticing Mercer standing off to the side.

"It's Leech," Kade began, but stopped when Lena nodded.

"Are we leaving now?"

"Yes. I've arranged transport in less than an hour. I'm sorry for making you get off one plane and onto another so soon, but there is a sense of urgency."

"I understand," Lena said. "I'll just use the facilities and collect my luggage."

"I'll get it," Mercer offered.

"Hello, Eighty-eight," she said to him, smirking.

"Don't start," teased Kade. "I've convinced them to stop calling you Barbie."

"Them? Surely you don't include Paps in that group."

"He does, Lena," Paps said, approaching them.

"Does this mean I have to call you Gunner?"

"Call me whatever you like, although it doesn't mean I'll answer." He leaned forward. "You look good, by the way."

The pretty pink flush that Kade remembered so well spread over Lena's cheeks as she returned Paps' smile. "Thank you," she murmured.

Razor had messaged earlier, saying they wanted to go see Leech too. The man was as much a second father to them as he was to Kade.

"Where's Merrigan?" asked Razor when Quinn and Lena walked away, presumably to use the restroom.

"She's taking a different flight," Kade told him.

"You two seem pretty tight."

Kade shrugged, not wanting to have this conversation at all, but particularly not in front of Lena.

Kade motioned for the rest of the group to go around the corner to where the woman at the information desk said they could find Leech. He stayed back, thankful no one had asked why. If his instincts were right, and they usually were, Merrigan was in the small alcove around the corner from the elevator bays.

He turned his back to the wall and crossed his arms. "Hello, Fatale. Hiding from someone?"

"Hi, um…no."

"There isn't any point in lying to me."

"I'm not lying, and I'm not hiding. I came to see Leech because I called and the nurse told me you hadn't arrived yet, and the flat I'm staying in is right around the corner. I was only in for a minute so I didn't wear him out."

"That is a very lengthy and detailed explanation," he said as he stepped closer, grasped her neck, and held her still to kiss her.

Damn, he loved the feel of her soft lips against his. For someone who wasn't big on public displays of affection of any kind, where Merrigan was concerned, Kade didn't care where they were; he simply couldn't keep his hands off her.

"I missed you," he murmured.

She laughed. "It's been, what, fifteen hours or so?"

"Fifteen minutes is too long for me to be away from you."

Merrigan laughed again. "Who are you?"

Kade laughed too. "I was just wondering that myself." He pulled her close enough to rest his hardness against her. "I'm insatiable when it comes to you."

"Perhaps you're just making up for lost time."

He'd certainly wondered that, but it didn't feel that way. Instead, it felt more like he was head-over-heels in love with her.

He brought his lips to hers and slid his tongue in when she opened her mouth to him. He reached down and grasped her bottom with both hands, then rubbed against her. "You didn't happen to pass by any supply closets, did you?"

"No, but as I said, the flat—"

"Kade?"

He pulled away from Merrigan and turned around to see Lena standing with her hands on her hips.

"Lena, this is Merrigan." He stepped aside to allow the two women to shake hands, sensing he was about to get an earful from at least one of them.

"Someone you met in the hallway?" she asked.

"Actually—" Merrigan began.

"This is the woman who not only saved my life, but your father's life too."

The statement had done what he'd hoped it would. While Lena still appeared pissed, at least she was no longer on the attack. Or so he hoped.

"My father is asking for you," she said to Kade, ignoring Merrigan completely, and wrapping her arm through his to guide him to the room.

Kade wriggled free from her grasp. "I'll be there in a minute," he said and motioned for Lena to beat it.

"I'm sorry," he said, reaching for Merrigan again.

"Don't be." She rolled her shoulders and yawned. "I'm exhausted. You go see Leech, who, by the way, seems to have taken a different turn and appears healthier than I've ever seen him. Although that's not saying much."

"I wonder what he's up to."

"That's the same thing I said to him."

"And?"

Merrigan shrugged. "You judge for yourself."

Kade watched Leech interact with Lena and Quinn, and agreed with Merrigan that he was up to something.

"Can I have a minute with my boys?" Leech asked a few minutes later.

"Tell me about Calder," he said once Kade closed the door behind Quinn and her mother.

"He's dead."

"I should've let you kill him twenty years ago," Leech murmured.

"As Quinn said to her mother before we got on the plane earlier, there is no future in our past. She also suggested we start over now and build new memories."

Leech looked between Paps, Razor, Mercer, and Laird, then back at Kade. "Who the hell are you?" he asked.

They all laughed, him included. "I've been asking myself the same thing."

"He's in love," Razor blurted.

The expression on Leech's face changed dramatically. "Who with?"

"Fatale," answered Paps.

"I see," said Leech, turning to Kade's father. "What's your take on this, Burns?"

"If what you're asking is whether I approve of my son and the MI6 agent, how can I not?"

"Meaning?" Leech asked.

"It isn't that different than how I met Sorcha."

Again Kade watched as Leech contemplated his father's answer.

Kade walked over to the door and held it open. "Would you excuse us, gentlemen?"

When the four other men left the room, Kade addressed Leech.

"What is this about?" he asked.

"Are you certain you aren't misleading Fatale?"

"In what way?"

"Falling in love with the woman who saved your life? Fairly classic, isn't it? So is the downward spiral once you realize it was never love at all, merely gratitude."

Kade sat in the chair near the bed, stunned by Leech's words. While it might be too early for him to say definitively that he was in love with her, particularly out loud, he certainly wasn't confused by why he wanted to spend time with her. It wasn't a want, actually. It was a need, and that had nothing to do with the fact that she'd rescued him.

"I'll ask you again. What is this about?"

When Leech refused to meet his eyes, it dawned on Kade what it might be.

"That ship sailed a very long time ago."

"Things could be different now, though. You said it yourself, or Quinn did. It's time to build new memories, to start over."

"Is this why you gathered us here to say 'goodbye'?"

Leech didn't answer, but Kade sensed his affirmation.

"I didn't think you'd bring the whole team with you."

Kade guessed Leech thought he'd bring Lena and Quinn, and the three would be a step closer to creating the happy family they'd never had before.

"It isn't going to happen, Leech," said Kade, as earnestly as he knew how. "Lena doesn't want it any more than I do."

"She's always wanted it."

"I don't agree. Maybe there was a time when she thought she did, but if she allows herself to take an honest look at the beginning of our marriage, she'd see, as well as I do, that the only reason we were together was for Quinn."

"I told you, once, not to break Lena's heart."

"Dad," came a voice from the doorway. "Kade didn't break my heart. Calder did, and not because I loved him. He broke all of our hearts with his betrayal. He was evil incarnate, and now, he's gone. While I hope I can move on with my life, knowing he no longer poses a threat to Quinn or me, that doesn't mean Kade and I can rekindle what was destroyed all those years ago."

She walked over and sat on the edge of the hospital bed. "You heard him. The only reason we were together was for Quinn."

"Not the only reason," murmured Kade.

Lena shrugged, but the look on her face broke Kade's heart. He wished he could take back what he'd said to her father, but only because she'd heard him, not because he didn't believe it was true.

"What have you told my granddaughter?"

"Nothing yet. She asked if I was her father, but the timing wasn't right for me to respond. Later, when I tried to talk to her about it, she wouldn't let me."

Lena turned to him. "What do you mean?"

"When Calder was holding Quinn hostage, Mercer tried to talk him down by telling him she was his daughter. After I put a bullet in his brain, I told her she was never his. She was always mine."

"Does she know about…?"

"I don't think so. As I said, whenever I've tried to discuss it with her, she wouldn't let me."

"I don't want her to know. I've never wanted her to know."

"We have to tell her something, Lena."

"Damn that Mercer."

"Sweetheart—" her father began.

"No, Dad. I'm not doing this." She glared at Kade before storming out.

"Big damn mess," Leech murmured. "I wish I could go back and change what happened."

"But then we wouldn't have Quinn."

Leech nodded. "By the way, what did you do, charter a plane?"

"Yep. You cost me a hell of a lot of money," said Kade, but with a smile on his face. "We'll go home that way too. Although when we do, you'll be with us."

"He needs his rest if he wants to leave this place," said the nurse entering the room. "No more visitors today, Mr. Hess," she scolded.

As Kade ushered everyone to the elevator a few minutes later, his father motioned him over.

"I'm going to stay a while longer."

"No problem, Da."

"Did I ever tell you I met your mother here?"

"You did." Kade smiled. He'd heard the story at least a hundred times.

"Spend time with them."

"What do you mean?"

"You and Merrigan have a lifetime ahead of you. Right now, Quinn needs you, and so does Lena, even if it isn't in a romantic way. Do this, son. You won't regret it. In fact, you'll thank me."

Kade heeded his father's words as he rode the elevator down with Paps, Razor, and Mercer. Lena and Quinn had gone ahead, saying there was a shop a few doors down they wanted to visit before it closed.

"Listen, I have a favor to ask. This will be hardest for you, Eighty-eight."

"Anything, Doc."

"I'd like to spend some time on my own with Lena and Quinn."

"Of course," Mercer murmured.

"No offense, but I think it will be easier for her to get to know me, and her mother, for that matter, if you're not there. She tends to look to you for approval."

"No offense taken, and I agree with you."

"It took her a while, but she eventually warmed up to me when Eighty-eight had to lay low for a couple of months," said Razor.

The only person who didn't say anything was Paps, but the scowl on his face said what words didn't.

"What's up?" Kade asked directly.

"Nothing," he muttered.

"You got something to say?"

"Hell, no. Whatever goes on with you, Barbie, and Skipper is none of my damn business." Paps looked between Mercer and Razor. "We're on our own tonight, boys. Where to?"

Kade made note of the restaurant they mentioned so he wouldn't show up there with Lena and Quinn. As he stepped out on the sidewalk, he vacillated between calling Merrigan and sending her a text.

Family dinner again tonight, he wrote. *I'll spare you.* It was the chicken shit way out, and he knew it.

He looked up and down the street, where he saw Lena and Quinn peering in a shop window. He walked over and stood between them, putting a hand on each of their shoulders. "How about I take my two girls to dinner tonight?" he asked, hoping Lena wouldn't ruin this moment with their daughter because she was angry with him.

Quinn looked behind him, obviously for Mercer.

"I requested it just be us tonight. Is that okay with you?"

"Of course. Um, can we stop by the hotel to freshen up first?"

Kade nodded, and they walked the two blocks to the hotel where he'd booked several rooms.

"I meant what I said, Kade. I don't want Quinn to know I was raped," Lena said after Quinn exited the elevator on her floor.

He nodded. "You're going to have to tell her something. I won't lie for you."

"You don't need to say anything at all."

It took them a minute to realize the elevator wasn't going anywhere because neither had hit the button for their floor. "Are you staying here as well?" Lena asked.

"Where else would I stay?"

"I thought maybe...never mind. What floor?"

Kade dug the envelope containing his room information out of his back pocket. "Ten."

"Oh," she said, hitting the corresponding button. "Me too."

Razor had checked them all in, apologizing that the rooms were scattered around the hotel rather than all on one floor. He'd handed out keys at the time, and Kade had stuck his in his back pocket, not bothering to look for his room number until now.

When the elevator stopped on the tenth floor, Kade waited for Lena to exit, hoping her room wasn't too close to his.

"I'm in 1014," she told him.

Kade was right next door. Later this evening, after they'd returned from dinner, he intended to find out exactly what Razor was up to. Maybe he was in cahoots with Leech and hadn't gotten the memo that neither he nor Lena had any interest in rekindling their relationship as anything other than friends, at least he hoped she didn't.

"Should we—" she said with her hand on the door.

"Let's meet in the lobby at nineteen hundred hours."

"Sounds fine. I'll let Quinn know."

He opened the door to his room and realized they hadn't discussed where they'd like to eat. If they were as tired as he was, they probably wouldn't care, but still, a gentleman would've at least asked what they were in the mood for.

Tomorrow night, he'd plan ahead and make a reservation. Tonight, they'd wing it. He opened his carry-on and grabbed a fresh shirt. He'd take a quick shower, then head downstairs. He'd be early, but it would give him a chance to have a drink and maybe even enough time to call Merrigan.

He checked his phone when he got in the elevator, like he had before he'd gotten in the shower, and again before he'd left his room, but there was still no response to the text he'd sent her. Maybe she'd decided to turn in early. They hadn't gotten much sleep the night before, and then with a twelve-hour flight, he was dragging himself.

He was partway through his beer when Lena joined him at the bar.

"What can I get you?" he asked.

"What are you having?"

"Hefeweizen."

"That's perfect. Quinn should be joining us shortly."

"Cheers," said Kade, when the bartender delivered Lena's beer.

"Cheers. Here's to…freedom."

"I know how hard these last few years have been for you."

"Last few years? How about my whole life? At least the part after the devil came to town."

"I wish I could've protected you from him. I still—"

"Don't," she snapped. "I know I brought it up, but I don't want to talk about anything to do with him or that night."

He took another drink of his beer and studied her over the rim of his glass. She was looking away from him, obviously fighting back tears.

What he'd started to say was true. He still dreamed of that night, more so when he was being held by the Russians. Each time he did, he made a different decision than the one he'd made twenty-two years ago.

He turned to the elevator and saw Quinn walking toward them. She looked so much like her mother had all those years ago. Thank God he'd been able to protect her from life's horrors. He only prayed he'd be able to continue to do so for the rest of her life. And if not him, Mercer.

Kade stood and held his arms open when Quinn approached, hoping that hugging him would become second nature when they were together.

"Hi," she said, accepting his hug.

"When you were little, you'd insist he give you a piggyback ride all around the house the minute he walked in the door," Lena said. "There were times I knew you were dead on your feet, but you never turned her down."

"I remember multiple laps, upstairs, downstairs, out on the patio, the driveway…" Kade laughed. "It was always as much fun for me as it was for you," he said, touching the tip of Quinn's nose with his finger. "You have the same smile," he said, looking between mother and daughter. "It's nice to see."

They had the same pink hue to their cheeks when they blushed too, but he didn't point that out. "I'm sorry I didn't ask earlier, but what are you two hungry for?"

"Anything," groaned Quinn. "I'm starving."

"There's a place called Emma's a short walk from here. It's casual, and they serve traditional German food," he suggested.

"Perfect," said Quinn, and then looked at her mother.

"Sounds good to me."

Kade motioned for the bartender, charged their drinks to the room, then led Lena and Quinn to the restaurant. Now that he was thinking about it, he was starving too, and Emma's had the best schnitzel—any kind a person could want—Jäger, Rahm, paprika, cream. It was one of his favorite places to eat, even though it bordered on fast food.

"Looks okay?" he asked when they walked in the door.

Quinn clapped her hands and ran over to the counter to look at what other people had ordered. "Oh my God. So much better than okay."

"Thank you," said Lena.

"For?"

"Tonight. Things are so…tentative between us. Your being here helps. Immensely."

"I'm sure there will be good days and bad as she navigates through her memories. All we can do is be here for her and answer her questions as best we can."

"Will you? Be here, I mean."

Kade set the menu he'd been looking at on the counter and faced Lena. "Yes. I will be. Once the dust of Calder's death settles and we get your dad back to the States, I'm retiring. Officially."

Lena raised her eyebrows. "For how long?"

Kade smiled. "I can assure you, after what we went through for the past two years, your father will be right there with me. In fact, maybe we'll take up fishing."

"What about your father? Didn't he retire several years ago?"

"My guess is there still isn't anyone who can beat Burns' record in terms of cleaning up well enough that no one knows the company was there." He wondered how much help the team had asked his father for while he'd been in captivity. Was he even aware that Calder was looking for something important enough to kill for it?

"What?"

"Nothing. A work thing."

"Retirement, huh?" She laughed, and so did he.

11

Merrigan

Merrigan had her hand on the door, but instead of opening it, she backed out of the way and peered in the window of Emma's, one of her favorite restaurants in this part of Germany.

There, in front of her, stood Kade, laughing and talking with his ex-wife. Every so often, she'd put her hand on his arm, then they'd nod and look into each other's eyes. She scanned the restaurant's tables, looking for signs of the "family dinner" he had spared her from, but only saw Quinn when she approached her parents, smiling in the same way her mother and father were.

What he'd done, actually, was spare her from a very *intimate* family dinner. One where an outsider of any kind wouldn't be welcomed into their family nucleus.

She continued to watch, much longer than she should've, as they walked to the counter, perhaps discussing what they'd have for dinner. When Kade rested his hand on his ex-wife's shoulder and squeezed, as he'd done with Merrigan at the family dinner she'd attended, she lost both her appetite and her willingness to continue torturing herself. She turned away and walked back to the hotel. Stupid, girly tears ran down her cheeks the whole way.

She was tired. More than tired, she was exhausted. That was the only explanation for her overreaction to seeing Kade with his…family. That's what they were. And no matter how much he thought he wanted to be with her every minute of the day, that was sex. Eventually, family would outweigh sex every time.

They'd spent one night together, and he was already sending her texts, making excuses for why he couldn't see her, even though they hadn't made plans.

Earlier, she was stunned that she'd somehow managed to arrive at the hospital before Kade and whoever else came with him.

When she'd entered his room, she found Leech in good spirits for someone who had been reported on death's door.

"What are you up to?" she asked, seeing him standing near the window.

"Fatale, it's good to see you, although it's somewhat of a surprise."

"I'm here because you've supposedly taken a turn. I'm to convince you life is worth living."

"Ramstein isn't such a bad place to visit, is it?"

"You're right, but you've got a crowd about to descend from America. I suggest you at least feign your turn for the worse."

Once he'd returned to bed, she leaned over and kissed his forehead. "You're warm," she mumbled, wondering when was the last time a nurse had checked his vitals. No sooner had she considered going in search of assistance than one came in.

"If you'll excuse us," she said to Merrigan.

"I was just leaving anyway. I'll be back later, Leech." She'd blown him a kiss and left. Now, she wished she'd waited until later to visit him and hadn't seen Kade at all.

She shook herself as if that would shake Kade out of her head. "You know better than this," she said out loud.

As tempted as she was to call Rivet again once she returned to her room, she knew he'd say the same thing he had before. She'd committed to the mission, and he expected her to see it through.

The quickest way to get Doc Butler out of her life for good would be to get her arse back to the States and find whatever Calder had been looking for, herself. Once she had, MI6 could decide how to use it to their advantage. She doubted very much they'd just hand it over to United Russia, even though they'd been the ones to help her infiltrate the Maskhadovs and eventually rescue Kade and Leech.

It didn't matter how many times Merrigan repeated in her head that it was exhilarating to be back in California, ready to scour every conceivable lead to find Calder's stash, as she'd begun thinking of it; she wasn't feeling it.

This was what she'd worked and trained for her whole life. She was in her element, never happier, right? Wrong. It was utter bullshit. She was miserable, and she had Kade Butler to thank for it.

As it turned out, one of the most helpful people she'd come across in the two days since she'd returned was Sorcha Butler. Yes, being around Kade's mother was a stab in the heart, but the woman was not only a mastermind; she was a former agent. It was Rivet who'd suggested Merrigan speak with her, and since she knew Kade was still in Ramstein, she wouldn't be risking seeing him.

"You should be running MI6," Merrigan said to her.

"Aye, lass. I should."

She laughed until Sorcha spoke again.

"Although it is not I who would be the first female chief, Merrigan. 'Tis you."

There'd been a time it was all she'd aspired to. But looking at it now, did she really want to sit at a desk day after day, puppeteering hundreds of operatives around the world? Traveling to every corner of the earth was one of the things she loved most about the career she'd chosen for herself. Although operating under the constant threat of danger ate away at her.

On the surface, her current mission didn't look all that dangerous or even mysterious. However, she knew United Russia had no real intention of abandoning the search for whatever Calder had been hiding.

The deal Kade had made with them was to return the double agent to them dead or alive—nothing was said or agreed upon in terms of what exactly they wanted Calder for, but everyone knew UR didn't want the man himself; they wanted what he had on them. If MI6 or the CIA found it first, they'd have the ultimate bargaining chip with the current Russian leadership.

It was a tossup as to who wanted it more. The UK's relations with Russia had been spiraling downward since the murder of a British-naturalized Russian defector and former officer of the Russian secret service who specialized in tackling organized crime.

MI6 had attributed the murder to FSB, the Federal Security Service of the Russian Federation, and had acted accordingly—freezing assets, ending intelligence cooperation, and expelling diplomats.

When another murder of a double agent occurred in the UK a few weeks ago, Anglo-Russian relations plummeted into their worst state in almost four decades.

Why did the UK care about United Russia? Because they controlled the government, which meant they also controlled exports of crude oil and gas. The UK and other EU countries were responsible for eighty percent of consumption, and without it, it would be a metaphorically cold day in her homeland.

What Merrigan couldn't figure out was why Calder couldn't find what he'd hid himself. Given its importance, could he really have forgotten where it was? The only logical answer was that someone else had found it. Who, though? And what had he or she done with it?

Merrigan smiled. Solving mysteries like this one was the part of the job she enjoyed the most. When she could let herself get lost in crafting a theory, she didn't think about the other things in her life as much.

When they met the following day, Sorcha told her the K19 team would be back later in the week and Leech would be with them.

While she'd grown to care about the man, feeling as though he'd manipulated her and the rest of his family into coming to say their "last goodbyes" pissed her off. Given his recovery was going well, Merrigan felt no guilt about not wanting to see him when he arrived in the States.

As far as Kade was concerned, out of sight meant out of heart had a better chance of working. She was MI6; he was former CIA, and they were both searching for the same thing. Whoever found it wouldn't necessarily be interested in sharing. It would serve her well to put the mission above all else—meaning, him.

"Don't avoid him, lass," Sorcha said, breaking through Merrigan's distraction as though she could read her mind.

"Sorcha, I…" She shook her head. "I have a job to do."

"Aye. A job."

She heard the accusation in Kade's mother's voice, however kindly it was delivered.

"I don't know what to say other than I think your son's interest is focused elsewhere."

"I *dinnae* believe that."

Soon, she would see for herself, just like Merrigan had the night she'd watched them through the window of what had once been her favorite restaurant in Ramstein, one she'd never be able to set foot in again without being reminded of how much it hurt to see Kade and Lena rekindling their romance of years ago.

"It was never love," Sorcha added. "He saved her."

"And I saved him."

Sorcha shook her head. "My Kade knows his heart. He's been waiting years for it to speak to him. Now that it has, he won't ignore what it's telling him."

"What about the other woman, Peyton? He was in love with her."

She shook her head again, this time more vigorously. *"Níl, tá tú mícheart."*

"Why do you say I'm wrong?"

"He saved her too."

Maybe that was the only way Kade knew how to love. He was a savior and protector by nature, which was a big reason he'd chosen a career in service to his country.

"We *dinnae ken* true love until we find it, lass. When we do, everything we believed before ceases to be."

"Is that how it was between you and Burns?"

Sorcha smiled. "Aye, lass. I knew the minute I laid eyes on him. Did you *ken* I was in Ramstein hospital?"

Merrigan shook her head.

Sorcha's eyes tightened. "Maybe there is something to loving a person who saved you."

"What do you mean?"

"'Twas Burns that saved my life, although I *dinnae ken* until several days later."

She went on to tell Merrigan that, as an agent, she'd infiltrated the Provisional Irish Republican Army, better known as the IRA. "I was at the Oxford Street bus station on Bloody Friday." Sorcha unfastened her blouse and showed Merrigan the scarring on her left arm and back. "I survived, but we lost two agents in the blast."

Merrigan was familiar with the events of that day. A total of twenty-four bombs were planted in and around the city of Belfast by the IRA, killing nine and injuring well over a hundred. At least seventy of those severely injured were civilian women and children.

"In a little over an hour, those bastards turned Belfast into a war zone."

"Why was Burns there?"

"The bombs had been detonating for over an hour when MI6 got the intel that a warning had been sent to the Royal Ulster Constabulary about another bomb scheduled to detonate at Oxford Street, the busiest bus station in all of Northern Ireland." Sorcha shook her head. "The two we lost refused to evacuate and were searching for the bomb when it went off." She stood and walked over to the window. "But you asked me about Burns, didn't you, lass?"

Merrigan nodded.

"He was part of the crew the agency sent in via heli. 'Twas him that carried me away from the blast."

"How did you end up in Ramstein?"

"He insisted I be transported there. I almost died several times due to infection, lass. If I'd stayed in Belfast, it would've killed me if the IRA didn't first."

"Your cover was blown."

"Aye," Sorcha repeated. "He saved my life in more ways than one." She patted Merrigan's hand. "That's enough about that."

Merrigan wanted to ask more, like what had happened between them at the hospital, how they'd ended up together, and how Kade had known his parents had been spies while none of his other siblings seemed to, but it was clear Sorcha didn't want to talk about it any longer.

"Will you come to dinner when they get home?"

Merrigan put her hand on Sorcha's, a gesture she rarely would have used, but she needed the woman to listen to what she was about to ask and, more importantly, honor her wishes. "I cannot. I hope you understand why."

"Aye, lass. And I *wull nae* interfere."

"I would appreciate it very much if you didn't."

Sorcha's eye hooded with guarded acquiescence.

Merrigan looked out the window of the house she'd rented in Cayucos, a town south of Cambria. It was a more densely populated area than the smaller seaside village, and this time, she'd been smart enough to use a new alias to secure both the house and car she was driving. If Sorcha kept her promise, it would be very difficult for Kade to find her.

"Who is 'Animus'?"

"I *dinnae ken*, but that is the code name the source referenced."

The intel Sorcha was passing on indicated that someone, code name Animus, was the one who'd found Calder's stash and had hidden it elsewhere. The name was not familiar to her, and the rudimentary search she'd done yielded nothing. She passed it on to her MI6 team, who could dig far deeper than she could.

It was the most promising lead she'd received and the only thing that made sense. Calder wouldn't have forgotten where he'd hidden the insurance he needed to keep the Maskhadovs from eliminating him.

"Who else has this information?" Merrigan asked Sorcha a few days later.

"Laird, and whoever else he's shared it with."

"Meaning the K19 team."

"I'm not certain, lass."

12

Kade

The struggle between wanting to keep Quinn all to himself to get to know her better and letting her get to know the side of her mother she'd never truly seen plagued Kade each of the last two mornings. It wasn't his decision; it was his daughter's, yet he sensed she was in as much of a quandary as he was.

Mercer offered to step aside several times in order to let them be alone, but Kade hadn't taken him up on it. Again, it was Quinn's decision to make.

Regardless of the question, she looked to his K19 partner for the answer before speaking. Mercer encouraged her to make her own decisions, but her hesitation each time was something Kade hoped she'd get past. Was it nervousness around him? Her mother? Or was that just the way Quinn was? If so, were he and Lena to blame?

Was her desire not to know whether he was her father another thing she was conflicted about? He hadn't attempted to have the conversation with her since arriving in Germany, but he didn't want to put it off any longer. It was important that she know.

The K19 team as well as Lena, Quinn, and his father had agreed to meet for breakfast every morning to map out a schedule for visiting Leech. While the man appeared in perfect health, the doctors and nurses remained guarded about his condition, particularly given his age and the trauma he'd endured the last two years. If he continued to improve, they predicted he'd be able to leave Ramstein within the week.

Kade wished it were tomorrow, or even today, but his desire to get back to the States had nothing to do with Leech. Instead, it was because he hadn't heard a word from Merrigan since he saw her at the hospital the first day they'd arrived. His countless calls and messages to her had gone unanswered. Finally, at his wit's end, he called her boss.

"What the hell do you mean she's back in the States?" Kade shouted through the phone.

"She left less than twenty-four hours after she arrived in Germany. Of course, she didn't go back straight away. She took a side trip to my office on her way to America," Rivet told him.

Sir Ranald "Rivet" Caird was a career British intelligence officer for the Secret Intelligence Service, also known as MI6. Three years ago, he'd been named chief. That Merrigan not only reported directly to him, but could walk into his office for an unscheduled meeting, meant something.

"She threatened to quit," Rivet added.

"Quit?"

"That's right."

What the hell had happened after she left the hospital, saying her flat was across the street and she was going to rest? It had to have been something earth-shattering to make her threaten to leave MI6 when she had to know she was being groomed to be Rivet's successor.

"She's my best bloody agent, Butler," Rivet barked. "Stay the hell out of her bed and let her do her job."

Kade wished it were that simple. He heard what Rivet was saying, but that didn't mean he could give up on her that easily.

Maybe her feelings for him weren't as strong as his were for her. Other than when she showed up with Paps and Razor, he'd been the one relentlessly pursuing her. Was he the reason she'd threatened to quit? He hadn't had the balls to ask Rivet directly.

She had a job to do, and she was damn good at it. That he and Leech were still alive was proof enough. God knew how many other ally agents she'd rescued from certain death while putting herself in as much or more danger than those she'd saved.

There was so much more to Fatale Shaw than bringing color to Kade's world. What an asshole he'd been, treating her as though all he cared about was getting her in his bed.

She had no idea how he really felt. It wasn't just color she brought; she gave his life meaning. While he still loved his country with every breath he took, he knew in his heart that, if he didn't already, one day he'd love Merrigan above all else.

They'd just ordered breakfast when Paps quietly suggested they have a meeting this afternoon to discuss their next course of action.

"There will be time for that on the plane ride home," Kade told him.

"Roger that." Paps grunted with a scowl.

He almost wished Paps would override him and call the meeting anyway. Kade had no more decision-making power at K19 than his other three partners did; it was just the role he fell into. Soon, though, that would change, given his plan to walk away from the company he'd founded alongside them.

His main reason for not wanting to meet with the team today was his determination to finally have a conversation with Quinn. He intended to ask her and Lena to stay behind once they'd finished breakfast. At first, he considered scheduling a time for them to talk privately; however, upon reflection, he changed his mind. It would be better to rip the bandage off quickly this morning rather than the three of them to be filled with anticipatory anxiety.

"It's time for us to talk," Kade began when Quinn and Lena followed him into his hotel room.

Lena looked ghostly pale. "Kade, please—"

"No, we're going to do this now. Have a seat," he said to both her and their daughter.

Kade took a deep breath, determined to get through this today and not let Lena or Quinn waylay him.

He pulled a chair close to where they were seated and leaned forward, resting his elbows on his knees. "This is not an easy discussion for any of us—"

He stopped talking when Quinn teared up.

"Let me finish, sweetheart," he implored, taking her hand in his.

She nodded.

"You are my daughter in every way that matters. That's the most important thing for you to remember."

"It's Calder, then," she murmured, looking between him and her mother.

"We don't know," said Kade, wishing Lena would say something.

Instead, she looked as though she was about to be sick to her stomach.

"What do you mean?" Quinn asked.

"We made a decision before you were born that knowing wouldn't change anything."

"You were…together, though?"

"Yes, sweetheart," he answered.

Kade waited for Lena to continue what he'd started. How much their daughter knew was up to her. It was her story to tell, not his.

No one wanted to forget the horrors of that night more than he did, except Lena, but their daughter deserved to know what had happened. Kade shuddered with the memory of it.

***

"Got a minute?" Leech asked when they were wrapping up their final day of training.

"Yes, sir," Kade said.

"Let's take a walk."

He followed Leech down the trail leading to the cabins where he and Calder had been bunking.

"We need to talk about Boiler."

Kade nodded. His quick temper had earned Calder the code name.

"Burns and I have decided he won't be reporting for duty with you next week."

"Shit," Kade muttered. While he wasn't surprised, the ramifications of that decision would be far-reaching for the man who had ended up as not only his bunkmate but, more and more, his nemesis. They'd left competitive behind weeks ago.

"We'll be talking with him later today, and while it isn't necessarily within the confines of your need to know, with the way things are between the two of you, I'm giving you a heads up."

"I appreciate it, sir."

"On to a more pleasant subject. What have you and Lena decided about the wedding?"

"Something small with just our parents, sir."

Given the nature of the job Kade had signed up for and was about to begin, they'd decided to keep the ceremony intimate, and the marriage under wraps for the time being.

"You might want to make yourself scarce tonight and give Boiler some space to pack his things and leave without an audience."

"Understood, sir."

***

There weren't very many days that went by when Kade didn't regret leaving the property that night.

"When my father told me Calder had been released from the program, I tried to console him, to offer my sympathy," he heard Lena say to Quinn. "He wasn't the first recruit who didn't make the team…"

"Mom, you don't have to do this. I know what happened."

The color left Lena's face as she looked between Kade and Quinn. *"How?"*

Kade was wondering the same thing.

"I saw the police report."

He was reeling as much as he knew Lena was, and while he tried not to react, he couldn't stop himself. "What do you mean you saw the police report?"

"It was with the things I found at the cabin. You know, with my birth certificate."

"Let's take a couple steps back. What exactly did you find, and where did you find it?"

Quinn explained she'd ran into Laird at her grandfather's place and that he'd told her he no longer owned it; his sons did. Then he'd given her permission to look around.

"I remembered a cabin my grandfather used to take me to on the west side of the property, so I went to see if I could find it. I did, and when I was about to leave, something caught my eye."

She told them how the wood floors were warped and that was how she'd discovered the box holding several documents—her birth certificate and the police report included.

"That was really all I paid attention to," she murmured. "There was a lot more, though."

"Where is it now?" Kade asked.

Quinn shrugged. "I don't know, but Mercer probably would."

"Why?" He shook with anger he was trying hard to control.

"Because he was there when I left. I assume he took it."

He turned to Lena. "What do you know about this?"

"Nothing," she said in a quiet voice.

"I'm sorry," said Quinn.

"There's nothing for you to apologize for," answered Kade. "My reaction…I was unaware…"

"It's okay," she mumbled, but he knew it wasn't.

His anger frightened her, and now, the tone of the conversation had changed.

He sat back down in the chair and leaned forward.

"I kept your letter," she told him.

What letter? Kade's mind raced, and then he remembered. "The trust."

Quinn nodded.

He couldn't remember exactly what he'd written, but he did recall telling her Naughton was the trustee and to contact him.

"In it, you said that you and my mother loved me very much."

"I meant it. It never mattered to me who your biological father was. You've always been *my* daughter."

She bit her lip and looked back and forth between Lena and him.

"Say it, Quinn," he coaxed.

"What if I want to know?"

He hadn't been prepared for that question, but he should have been. If he were in her shoes, he would ask the same thing.

"Lena, do you have anything to say?"

"Quinn, I'm not sure—"

"*You* don't have to be sure," she snapped at her mother, displaying more emotion and tenacity than he'd seen to that point. Oddly, he was proud of her.

Lena's behavior, though, bothered him. He understood her not wanting Quinn to know about the rape and maybe not wanting to know whether Calder was Quinn's biological father, but it wasn't just that. Something more was going on, and Kade couldn't put his finger on what it was.

13

Kade

"You get your wish, but I don't think you're gonna like it very much," Kade said when Paps answered his call.

"Oh yeah? What wish is that?"

"I'm calling an emergency meeting. *Now.*"

"What the—"

"Now," he repeated. "I'm in 1016. Tell Eighty-eight and Razor to get their asses over here too."

"Roger that." Paps disconnected the call.

Kade threw his phone on the bed, relieved that Paps hadn't pushed the issue and given him any more shit. He was already spitting mad.

"What's up?" Razor asked, coming in ahead of Paps and Mercer.

"Close the fucking door," Kade spat. Once it was shut, he motioned toward the chairs near the window. "Have a seat, gentlemen."

The other two sat, but Paps stood with his arms folded. "I'll stand. Now, tell us what this bullshit is all about."

"I had to find out from my *daughter* that she found certain documents in the floorboards of one of the cabins on Leech's property. Any of you want to explain why I wasn't briefed on that particular development?"

When the three men looked at one another, the answer became clear to him. "You all assumed someone else told me?"

"I'll take this one, Doc," said Mercer. "I should've briefed you."

"Nah, you're not taking this one, Eighty-eight," said Paps. "*You* are." He pointed at Kade.

"*What—*"

"Yeah, that's right. *You are.* It's been five *fucking* days since we saw your face for the first time in two years. We've been in the air most of that, and on top of that, you've *refused* to have the meetings I've requested. So don't give me, or them, any shit about what you were or weren't briefed about."

Kade gripped the back of his neck and turned away from them. To a certain extent, he agreed, but what

Quinn had found was important enough that they should've insisted.

"I know what you're thinking," Paps continued. "But don't assume for a hot minute that you can crawl into any of our heads and do the same."

"You're right, but—"

Paps stormed across the room and got in his face. *"Do you not get we were sure you were dead? Jesus Christ, Doc."*

By their look, Razor and Mercer were as stunned by Paps' outburst as he was. Kade had known the man for close to twenty-five years, and he'd never seen the level of emotion his teammate was exhibiting now.

"I don't know what to say," Kade murmured. It was as honest an answer as he could come up with. "Don't leave," he said when Paps walked to the door.

"I gotta. I'll catch up with you guys later," he muttered before letting the door close behind him.

"What the hell?" asked Mercer, looking at Razor, who shook his head.

"I don't know for sure…"

"But?" said Kade.

"I think this might have something to do with Barbie. And you."

"In what way?"

"You've been spending a lot of time together."

"For Quinn's sake."

"Yeah, well…"

"But he detests her," said Mercer.

"Maybe. Then again, maybe not."

"Holy shit," Mercer muttered, then looked at Kade.

"It isn't just that," said Razor. "You're back, and I just wonder if he's questioning his role in the organization."

He decided now was as good a time as any to tell them his plans. "I'm leaving K19. This will be my last mission."

"What?" the men said in unison.

"You heard me."

"You better find Paps and tell him, man. You should've told him first," said Razor. "You're pissed we didn't brief you on the info Skipper found? I gotta tell you…this feels worse."

Kade looked across the aisle of their chartered plane to where Quinn slept with her head on Mercer's shoulder. The last few days had to have been rough on her. He doubted he could've handled learning everything she had with as much grace and maturity.

Things hadn't been easy between Paps and him either. When Kade told him he intended to leave K19, the man had stormed off again, only to come back a few minutes later to tell him neither he nor Razor and Mercer were willing to accept his resignation until after they'd completed their current mission. Once they had, it would be up to the four of them together to determine whether K19 would stay in business or dissolve completely.

"It's all or none," Paps had said. "You better be damn sure you want to quit, because if you do, we do too."

Leech approached and sat in the seat across from him on the same side of the plane in a row that faced the back. "Lena said you told her," he whispered.

Kade nodded. "She needed to know."

"What now?"

"She and I will arrange for a DNA test."

"And what if—"

Kade leaned forward, speaking as quietly as he could. "I'll tell you the same thing I told her. I'm her father. It doesn't matter what any test says. If it were up to me, we wouldn't do it. But it isn't up to me. It's her decision."

He thought about how Quinn struggled with that very thing, always looking to Mercer for his opinion before voicing her own. She'd come to this decision without his input or anyone else's, and no matter how hard it was to consider the outcome, he would respect her wanting to know.

He cringed when he saw Quinn stand. "I'm sorry if we woke you."

"May I?" she asked, motioning to the seat next to her grandfather.

"Of course," he said, moving aside the papers and blanket he'd set there.

She sat and faced him. "I know you and Mom don't want me to do this." She took a deep breath. "I can't explain it, but I have to know."

"It's okay," said Kade, immediately wishing he hadn't when he saw the look on her face.

"I don't care whether anyone else thinks it's *okay*."

Kade held up his hands and did his best not to smile. "Got it."

"Poppy…" she began and hesitated as though she was stunned by the word. "Is it okay if I call you that?"

Leech smiled. "Always."

"It's what I used to call you, isn't it?"

"It is. Do you remember what you called your grandmother?"

"Nonna."

"That's right," he said with a huge smile.

Quinn, however, was more somber. "I know so little about my own life, Poppy. Even if you don't agree with my decision, please respect it."

Leech was quiet for a while and looked out the window. When he turned back to face them, his expression had changed. "I will, Quinn. You'll hear no further argument from me," he vowed.

Kade looked over to where Quinn had been sitting and met Mercer's eyes.

He looked as exhausted as Kade felt. He imagined they all were. The ten days since Calder's death had been an emotional roller coaster for everyone.

"The seat next to Lena is vacant," Leech said after Quinn went back to hers.

When he wiggled his eyebrows, Kade almost lost it. No matter how clear he'd continued to be about not being interested in a relationship with Lena, Leech remained relentless. Once they landed and Kade could get his former mentor alone, he intended to make it clear the subject was closed.

"Yeah? Why don't you go sit there?" he said instead.

Kade's foul mood wasn't related solely to Leech's annoying suggestions. He was also becoming increasingly agitated about his inability to connect with Merrigan. She hadn't responded to his texts or messages despite Rivet's assurance that they had daily communication.

"Da," Kade greeted him when his father came and sat with Leech and him.

"Before you meet with your team again, there's something I want you to be aware of."

Kade nodded.

"What Calder was looking for, and I'm assuming your team is as well…"

"Go on, Da," he urged.

"I believe I have information that will prove useful to your search. We may have a lead…"

"How long have you held onto this?" Kade didn't even attempt to mask his irritation.

His father looked him in the eye. "I received the intel shortly before we left Germany."

"Interesting," said Leech, "But I don't think now is the time to discuss it."

"I agree," said Kade.

The only two people on the plane he'd rather not have this conversation in front of were Quinn and Lena. Quinn appeared to have fallen back to sleep, but Kade had no idea whether Lena was within earshot, and he had no intention of looking.

He'd been consciously avoiding spending time with her unless it was as a family, particularly since Lena had invited him into her hotel room a couple of nights in a row for an "after-dinner drink." He'd declined both times, and while she'd tried to play it off as no big deal, he saw the hurt in her eyes at his rejection. When it happened for the third time last night, he'd told her they needed to talk and asked her to come back down to the lobby with him. She'd told him it wasn't necessary; she was trying to be friendly, and he didn't need to make such a fuss about it.

He closed his eyes and let his mind drift away from Lena and to Merrigan. He missed her, which wasn't a feeling he'd experienced very often.

He'd missed Peyton when they were together and he'd leave on a mission, but it had never felt as strong as the yearning he now felt for Merrigan.

Write her a letter. He heard the words spoken in his mind as though they were said by someone else. It was a good idea, though. That way, he could tell her how he was feeling without stalking her. If, after reading it, she still didn't contact him, he'd know it was time to let go.

Kade stood and walked to the back of the plane, where there were two staterooms.

"I have some work to catch up on," he said when he passed Lena and she raised a brow.

She nodded when he walked through the door and locked it behind him, thankful she hadn't made a move to come in with him.

He sat down and pulled the writing paper he always carried with him out of his briefcase and thought about what he wanted to say.

Dear Merrigan,

It has been over a week since I last saw your face, heard your voice, and was blessed with the warmth having you near brings. It's been even longer since I held your naked body next to mine.

With every passing minute, I miss you more. Every thought I have is filled with you, wheth-er it's because I can't wait to share something with you or simply hold you in my arms. The only time I can do either is when I close my eyes and imagine you're with me.

I wish I knew what happened to make you leave Ramstein so abruptly, and why, since, you haven't answered my calls or texts. I so wish you would've felt like you could share whatever it was with me.

The world is dull and gray without you near, my sweet Merrigan. Only days ago, everything in my world was vibrant and alive, but only because you shone your magnificent light on all that surrounds me.

I am on a flight to the States as I write this. I will figure out a way to get it delivered to you once we land, but I will not attempt to see you myself until you tell me it's what you want. You, of all people, know how difficult that will be for me, but that is how much I care about you—enough to wait for your decision and not impose my desires onto you.

Only moments ago, I realized I have hesitated to tell you how I feel, and I don't know why.

Habit, perhaps. But I can't hold back any longer. You are my sunrise and sunset, the person I want to be with every moment of every day. You're the music in my ears and the joy in my heart.

Please let me back into your life.

With great love and respect,
Kade

He closed his eyes and pictured her naked before him and the way her eyes had bored into his when their bodies joined together. He'd wanted to tell her how he felt then, but fear had stopped him, and he regretted it now.

He'd found the woman he wanted forever with, and he had to overcome his self-imposed obstacles in order to be with her. Whatever it took, he'd do. Whatever she wanted, he'd deliver.

It had taken him a long time to find the other half of his soul, and now that he had, he hoped she wouldn't force him to let her go.

The rest of the flight had gone from bad to worse. By the time they landed, he wasn't the only one in a foul mood. His every instinct screamed at him to get away, even if just for some good old-fashioned R and R.

He couldn't go anywhere yet, though, the team still had to meet and discuss the intel his father had received and, from there, find Calder's damned files.

"Does the name Animus mean anything to any of you?" his father asked him, Paps, and Razor once they'd confirmed Lena, Quinn, and Leech had gone in search of restrooms.

"Who searched the cabins after Quinn's discovery?" Kade asked.

"Eighty-eight at first, but then I did another sweep," answered Razor.

"Are you saying you didn't put the files in the floorboards?" asked Mercer.

Kade shook his head. "What all was there?"

"Not a whole lot. You already know about Quinn's birth certificate and the police report. The rest were an odd collection of things. Mainly training reports. Some were yours, some were Calder's. Everything else was random. Some receipts that were so faded we couldn't read them," Paps told him.

"Where had you been keeping it?" asked Razor.

Kade rubbed his chin. "Some of it was at the house in Montecito, but it wasn't all together. The letter, for example, I could've sworn I put that in the safe-deposit box. Some of it doesn't even sound familiar."

"We all emptied the contents of the safe box together, Doc. There were several letters, but only one that wasn't addressed to anyone, and that one was with Ainsley's letter."

"Did you give it to Ains?" Kade asked Mercer.

"I did," answered his father. "On Christmas."

"Where is it now?"

Mercer shrugged. "Who was it for?"

"Quinn."

"She hasn't mentioned it."

Quinn had found his letter about the trust before Ainsley received hers at Christmas, but that didn't really matter. The first he wrote—the one she'd already read—while full of mystery, was intended to make sure she knew he'd set up the trust on her behalf.

The second was more personal. In it, he'd told her about his family and how he hoped she'd allow them into her life. He wrote about his favorite memory of each of his siblings and told her that, no matter what, she was his daughter and always would be. He hadn't decided yet whether he ever wanted her to read it. So much of it was redundant at this point.

"What are you thinking?" Paps asked.

"Since I didn't put those documents in the cabin's floorboards, who did?"

"Any ideas?"

"I'm thinking—" Kade began.

Paps shook his head and motioned with his chin.

"Kade?" said Lena, standing behind him.

"Yes?"

"Can we talk for a minute?"

He motioned for her to take a seat. "What can I do for you?"

"I was thinking we could spend some time at the house now that we're back."

Did she mean Casa Carrizo in Montecito? He'd already given thought to inviting Quinn and Mercer to join him, so his daughter could spend more time in the house where she'd lived her first seven years. Extending the invitation to Lena hadn't been part of his plan.

The bottom line was the house was his, but could he deny her access to it? He might've if he hadn't ended

up owning half of what had been her family's estate—
land that now belonged to two of his brothers.

"We'll talk more about it later."

"Later, when? Do you realize I don't have anywhere
to go when we leave this airport?"

"That isn't true, and you know it."

"Are you suggesting I stay at the house in town with
my father?"

"Lena…"

"You are, aren't you?"

"Are you kidding me right now?" he said quietly
enough that he hoped only she could hear him.

"I thought I could stay at Casa Carrizo."

"That isn't a good idea."

"Why not?"

"As I said, we'll talk more about it later."

"I need a place of my own."

"Find one."

Where she lived wasn't his problem, and with the
Calder threat neutralized, she could go anywhere she
wanted to. It was only misguided guilt over the land his
two brothers now owned that made him feel remotely
benevolent in the first place.

It had been a long time since he thought about the day he discovered it was his.

***

"What is this?" Kade asked Leech when he handed him an envelope.

"Peter Wendt scheduled the reading of Elisabetta's will." The usually stoic man's voice was shaky, and while Kade didn't want to be disrespectful, he wasn't sure what that had to do with him.

"Open it." Leech pointed to the envelope.

He did and saw the letter inside was addressed to him, requesting his attendance at the reading. If for some reason he wasn't able to attend, it would be rescheduled.

"I don't understand."

"You will."

Two days later, Kade sat in a room with Leech and Lena and listened as the family's attorney told him Elisabetta had left him half of what had once been called the Demetria Estate. Neither Leech nor Lena looked surprised.

"I can't accept this," he said, stunned.

"If you refuse the inheritance, it will be divided equally among the five of your siblings," Peter told him.

"Why?"

"It's what my mother wanted," Lena answered.

Kade wasn't sure what to say.

"I'll give you a minute," Peter offered. He left the room before they responded.

"Why did she do this?" Kade asked Leech directly once they and Lena were alone.

"As my daughter said, it's what her mother wanted. The property has never been mine, son. It's always been Elisabetta's."

California was a community property state, which meant that upon her death, the estate should've passed directly to Leech. Only her specifically stated intent to divide the property would supersede the default inheritance. Kade looked between Leech and Lena.

"Who owns the rest?"

"I retain ownership of the balance," answered Leech. "The vineyards could be brought back, making it a lucrative wine-producing property," he added.

Kade looked at Lena, who appeared nonplussed. This land was her birthright not his; he'd simply accept it and use a quitclaim deed to give it to her.

"You may give it to your siblings, but otherwise, you may not deed the property to anyone else. The codicil is clear," Leech said, as though he anticipated Kade's plan.

"This isn't right," Kade said emphatically. "I'll discuss this with my own attorney, and we'll get this straightened out. I'm sorry, Lena."

"Why are you apologizing to me?"

"Because this land should stay in your family."

"She considered you part of our family."

Kade scrubbed his face. Was that what Elisabetta had hoped, that he and Lena would reconcile, and thus, the land would stay in the family? If so, it was manipulation on the grandest scale, and he couldn't abide it. He and Lena had been married, and it hadn't worked out. The circumstances he attributed to the demise of their union hadn't changed. There was no way Kade would consider remarrying or entertain the idea of a romantic relationship with her, even if he were single.

"Excuse me," he said, standing so abruptly his chair threatened to overturn. He righted it and stalked out of the office, determined to find a legal way to undo what Lena's mother had done.

"Hold up a minute," Peter said when Kade passed him on his way out.

"I'm hiring my own attorney," he said to the man who, as a former operative, had been a trusted colleague.

"Don't bother."

"With all due respect—"

"It's ironclad. She made sure of it."

"To get me to remarry Lena? It isn't happening."

"She may have had other reasons."

Kade raised an eyebrow. "Seriously, Rawhide?" He used the man's former code name, reminding him of the loyalty he expected, given their prior relationship.

"Maybe she had other reasons."

"Like what?"

Peter shook his head. "I really can't say."

"This is bullshit."

***

Even now, Kade was angry about the whole thing. He felt manipulated regardless of whether he'd capitulated or not. He shook his head again, vowing not to let Lena continue playing on his guilt about the inheritance. There were plenty of other things, where she was concerned, that he felt bad about.

14

Merrigan

Given the plane Kade had been on landed almost seventy-two hours ago, Merrigan felt confident her plan to prevent him from finding her had proved successful. It also confirmed Sorcha had kept her word not to interfere by divulging her location.

When she saw the post deliverer approach her house with what could only be another slew of trash mail she felt terribly guilty. Every day when it arrived, she merely stuffed it into the rubbish bin.

She picked it up off the floor beneath the mail slot in the front door and walked into the kitchen to toss it, then make herself a pot of tea.

As she dumped the pile of circulars into the bin, something caught her eye. She sifted through the stack until she found the white envelope she'd spotted.

It was addressed to her in what looked like Sorcha Butler's handwriting. Wondering what she was up to, Merrigan grabbed a knife and sliced the envelope open. The letter she found inside was written in a different script.

When the kettle whistled, she set the piece of paper on the table, poured the hot water over the tea bag, then read the words Kade had written to her over and over again.

The world is dull and gray without you near, my sweet Merrigan.

She understood what he meant. Her world, too, was dull and gray without him near.

Please let me back into your life.

What could she say when he implored so sweetly? God, help her, but she couldn't resist Kade Butler, no matter how hard she tried. The safety net of him being in a different country, halfway around the globe, had been pulled from beneath her, and here she sat, vacillating between calling or messaging him. The only thing she couldn't do was continue to shun him, not after the heartfelt words he'd written to her.

15

Kade

Kade had practically gotten on his hands and knees and begged his mother to tell him where Merrigan was. It was Da who'd told him Sorcha worked with her while they were in Germany.

Over and over, she'd refused until Kade finally held his folded letter in front of her. "I've written this to her, to tell her how I feel."

Still, she wouldn't give in until he succumbed and let her read it. When she turned the paper over and finished reading his words, tears in her eyes, he knew she'd help him.

"I'll post it to her," she agreed. "But *dinnae* ask me for more."

Kade thanked her and didn't say anything else because that was all he'd really wanted. He hoped that once Merrigan read his words, she'd at least agree to see him.

It took two days, but Kade had finally gotten Lena to give up on staying at Casa Carrizo. He wasn't certain, but something told him Paps had interceded and convinced her to relent.

He was the one to tell Kade she'd rented a house in Summerland, a town less than fifteen minutes away from Montecito.

His intention, now, was to head to Casa Carrizo as soon as he heard from Merrigan. He hoped she'd go with him, but if not, that was where he'd go to lick his wounds.

He picked up his phone to check for messages, not expecting any, but there it was, the text he'd been waiting for.

Thank you for your beautiful letter, she wrote.

I meant every word, he responded. *Can I please see you?*

It took several minutes for her to answer, but when she did, she asked if she could come to him.

I'm at the ranch.

See you at 1400.

Kade checked the time. Four more hours. He hoped he could last that long without pacing a hole in his floor.

He was tempted to contact Quinn and Mercer about going to Montecito with him, but forced himself to wait. His daughter was the most important person in his life right now, but Merrigan was a close second. His priority today was to fix whatever had gone wrong between them, so he could focus on the rest of his life. As it was, she was all he could think about.

After an hour, Kade sent a message to Naughton, asking if he could ride his horse, Huck. The old draft horse was one of the few he felt comfortable on, other than Brodie's Morgan, which was now stabled at his and Peyton's house on See Canyon Road.

"Huck's saddled and ready to go," Naughton called and told him.

"I could've done that."

"You can cool him down."

"Fair enough, Naught. Thanks."

"Kade?"

"Yeah?"

"I sure am glad you're back."

"Me too, brother."

It had been a long damned time since he'd ridden the ranch. More years than he could remember. When he'd come home before, he'd stick around for a couple of days, get caught up with his family, then be ready to leave again.

It was different when he met Peyton, but even then, he didn't stay at the ranch. After they'd been seeing each other for a few months, he started staying at her place instead.

He'd still find reasons to take off and be on his own for a while, which she'd always been good about. Peyton was as independent as he was, or she had been. It seemed as though she and Brodie had settled into a really nice life for themselves and the boys.

He couldn't believe how much Jamison and Finn had grown when he saw them at his parents' dinner.

It had been that way with Quinn. Every time he received another batch of photos of her, he couldn't believe how much she'd changed. It broke his heart not being able to watch it happen up close.

Whenever he returned from a mission, he'd be summoned to Langley before he could go back to the West Coast, and each time, he scheduled a side trip to New York, if only to catch a glimpse of his daughter.

Maybe that was why he felt so off. He'd always been alone when visiting Manhattan, so whatever shit he had to process through or demons he had to exorcise, he did before he came home, in the comfort of his favorite hotel, the Mandarin.

He'd book the Oriental Suite, with a view of Central Park, order room service when he didn't feel like going out, and walk the city when he did.

Maybe Merrigan would like to visit it with him. He'd bet she'd love the bird's-eye view of the park from high above Columbus Circle.

Kade shook his head and laughed at himself. There had never been a woman he remotely thought of taking to the place he considered his private respite, but once again, she was at the forefront of his thoughts, no matter the subject.

He was almost back to the barn when he saw a sleek, Corris gray Jaguar F-Type Coupe pulling through the ranch gates.

He dismounted, let Huck loose in the pasture, and closed the gate behind him.

Kade waved when he saw it was Merrigan driving and waited while she parked. He was halfway to her when she climbed out of the car. The breeze in her hair took his breath away, and the way her tight sweater hugged her curves set the rest of his body on fire. He had no restraint when it came to this woman. He could spend all day, all night, and every day after that with her and still never get enough.

The sun was bright and reflecting on the car's windshield, so she shielded her eyes and looked in his direction.

"Hi." She waved.

He got close enough to grasp her nape with his hand and look into her eyes. "It's so good to see you."

Merrigan leaned into his hand and closed her eyes. "You wrote me a beautiful letter," she said with the Scottish lilt that had first made him think she was an angel.

"I told you before I meant every word. It was the only way I knew to tell you how I feel, both when I'm with you and when I'm not."

"I have to admit," she murmured. "I don't like being away from you, either."

Kade took her hand in his and led her away from the car. "Nice ride, by the way."

"I was feeling…adventurous."

"It suits you."

When they got several feet away from it, she let go of his hand. "Should I park somewhere else?"

He turned around and snaked his arm around her waist, getting close enough that their lips almost touched. "No," he said, before giving her a scorching kiss.

She smiled. "I love it when you do that."

"I'm happy to do more of it." He kissed her again, deeper and harder. "I can't get enough of you; no matter how many times I kiss you or hold you close to me, it'll never be enough." He leaned back so he could look into her eyes. "If you're not feeling the same way I am, Merrigan, you need to tell me now, because I'm all in with you. Do you understand?"

She breathed deeply and nodded. "I could say the same about you."

"Thank God," he said, leading her to the winery.

She didn't ask where he was taking her, only followed, her hand in his.

They climbed the stairs to his apartment, and he kicked open the door with the toe of his boot. As soon as they were inside, he closed the door behind her, then swept her up in his arms.

Kade carried her into his bedroom and stood next to the bed, not wanting to release her. "I want to feel you next to me, not just now but always."

"Kade…"

"Please tell me you want the same thing."

"I do, just with fewer clothes."

He set her on her feet and pulled her deep-amethyst sweater over her head and tossed it to the closest chair. Before her fingers could undo the button on her jeans, he moved her hands away. "Let me," he whispered, slowly opening the zipper, then tucking his hands inside and lowering her pants to the floor.

Kade knelt before her and kissed across her body just above the fiery red curls of her sex. He breathed in the scent of her and groaned with want.

Merrigan's hands rested on his shoulders, and she arched her back. When he leaned forward, scattering more kisses, she moaned.

"Let's lose these, baby," he told her, holding her steady as she stepped out of the jeans puddled near her ankles. "Open for me," he said, resting his hands on the inside of her thighs until she'd spread her legs far enough for him to see and taste her want for him.

16

Merrigan

How many times had she dreamed about Kade making love to her body? What he was doing to her now felt better than any fantasy she'd had, awake or asleep. Her fingernails dug into the skin on his shoulders as she struggled to remain standing.

"Stay still for me," he said, grasping her bottom with both hands and holding her where he wanted her.

"Kade, I…God…" His mouth brought her to an orgasm unlike any other she'd had, except with him. Only Kade could coax such ecstasy from her.

He stood, taking her weight and sweeping her to the bed, where he stood and trailed his eyes down her body. After shedding his own clothes, Kade opened the drawer of the nightstand and pulled out a foil packet. "I wish we didn't have to have anything between us, Merrigan."

She took the foil from his hand and tossed it on the floor. "We don't."

"Are you sure?"

"Yes. I've been on birth control for years, and I haven't been with anyone…"

"Neither have I."

"You didn't…"

He held himself above her. "Finish what you were going to say."

"No."

"I will not touch another part of your body with mine until you do."

She looked away, but he waited.

"Say it, dammit."

"Were you with her?" she whimpered, hating the jealousy and doubt in her own voice.

"Look at me."

She turned her head and looked into his eyes.

"No. I wasn't with Lena or anyone else. And I won't be. Not ever again if I have my way."

Her eyes stayed focused on his as she felt his hardness breach her sex. His mouth came down on hers, and he slipped his tongue between her lips. Kade kissed her, softly at first, and then harder as the frenzy of their need grew.

"I love the way you feel, wrapped around me," he breathed, thrusting harder and harder until she couldn't hold back any longer.

When the pleasure he wreaked on her body built to a crescendo, Merrigan felt as though she was soaring. "Come with me," she moaned, wanting him to fly as high as she was.

Merrigan rested her head on Kade's chest and listened to his heart beating in time with her own.

"Do you have any idea how important you are to me?" he asked.

"I'm beginning to."

"There's something we need to talk about."

"Okay."

"The Animus intel."

"Right." She had planned to bring it up to him, but not while they were naked in each other's arms.

"We need to come to an agreement, because this"—he squeezed her—"is what is most important to me."

"Above your commitment to your country?"

Kade was quiet for a couple of minutes. Merrigan would have an equally difficult time answering such a question. Regardless of how powerful their feelings seemed, this thing between them was so new.

"I want us to come to an agreement that will allow us to honor our commitment to our respective agencies, but also honor our relationship."

"What if those agencies are unwilling to sign off on our personal agreement?"

"We do it anyway."

Therein lay the rub. How could she agree to honor her commitment in one way, but not the other? It was easier for Kade; he was an independent contractor. While he had to abide by whatever his contract stated, it wasn't the same as her refusing to do her job. Agreeing to a side deal was paramount to treason, in essence.

"I can speak to Rivet if you'd like."

Did he really just suggest he speak to her boss on her behalf? Merrigan bristled.

"Hear me out."

She sat up and turned so she was looking at him.

"I would suggest a deal between the CIA and MI6. If we find whatever Calder had on United Russia first, we agree to share it with MI6. And vice versa."

"You can't make that decision."

"No, but I can make the recommendation."

"And if the CIA refuses to agree?"

"Then I try a different negotiation tactic."

"And if I find it before you do?"

"My proposal is that you and I agree to continue to work together."

"We get *permission* to continue to work together."

"Semantics, sweetheart."

It was a possibility. When she'd gone in undercover, it was to infiltrate the Maskhadovs. The fact that they held two Americans captive became part of a negotiation between MI6 and the CIA. Rescuing them hadn't been her original intent. Could this be considered a continuation of that mission?

"I need to talk to Rivet myself."

"Okay." Kade pulled her down next to him. "I don't want anything to come between us, Merrigan. That's my point."

"What about future missions? While MI6 and the CIA have historically worked together for certain things, we have also gone our separate ways on more than one occasion."

"There won't be future missions for me."

"Why not?" she asked.

"Once I've seen this through to the end, I'm retiring."

"And doing what?"

"I haven't figured that out yet."

"I see."

"I'm going away for a few days to think about it. Maybe longer," he said, pulling her tighter to him. "I'd like you to go with me."

"Kade, I…"

"Think about it. Where I'm going isn't that far away. It's a little over two hours from here."

"What about Animus?"

"Paps and Razor will continue working the lead. Maybe Mercer too, but my intention is to ask Quinn and him to join me."

"I know you said it's two hours from here, but where exactly?"

Kade told her about the house in Montecito. He'd originally purchased it for the privacy and ease of securing the property.

"I love its proximity to the ocean, as well as the small-community feel of the town. Not to mention the house and grounds are breathtaking. The house, Casa Carrizo, is named for the reeds that grow on the bank of the stream running through the property."

Kade hadn't said it specifically, but Merrigan surmised he'd purchased the house for Lena, Quinn, and him to live in. "It's your house, then?"

"Yes. All mine." He cleared his throat. "Why did you leave Germany?" he asked.

Merrigan's body tensed. "There were a number of reasons."

"What were they?"

"I have a mission to complete, Kade, and being manipulated to visit Leech's bedside derailed me. He never intended for me to be included in his summons in the first place. He wanted you, his daughter, and his granddaughter there. He was blindsided when I first showed up."

"You and I spoke after you saw him. You acknowledged his subterfuge, but said nothing about returning to the States on the next flight out."

"I changed my mind."

"Why?"

"I don't see how this is your concern. I made a decision to return, and that's what I did."

Kade turned his body so they were face-to-face. "Stop lying to me, and tell me why you left."

When she tried to get up, he stopped her.

"Tell me what happened, Merrigan."

"I saw you."

"Where?"

"At Emma's. Remember the family dinner you so nobly spared me from? I saw your familial reunion and realized that, perhaps, I should step away so as not to ruin your evening with your wife and daughter."

"Ex-wife."

"Whatever."

"No, not whatever. At one point, Lena was my wife. We divorced. There is no chance she and I will ever be together again."

"That's what you say, but what I saw indicated otherwise."

"What you saw was three people very tentatively trying to spend family time together. The memories we shared were for Quinn's benefit."

This time when Merrigan tried to move away, he let her, and she turned her back to him.

"My life is not designed for relationships. Of any kind, including my family. You, of all people, should understand that," she said.

"Look at me."

When she refused and he didn't repeat his request, Merrigan knew he had no intention of dropping the subject. Instead, he'd wait. All night if necessary.

"That was harsh. I'm sorry," she murmured, turning to face him.

"There is one thing you were absolutely right about. I do understand, and before I met you, I would've recited the same speech. I feel differently now, and I don't intend to give you an out. I won't tell you to walk away if you don't feel the same way I do. Instead, I'm going to ask you to give us a chance. Spend time with me away from the work we do."

"Kade, I—"

"Please, Merrigan. I *know* you're feeling the same things I am. No matter how deep you try to bury it. Now, get back in bed, woman." When he smiled and held his hand out, she smiled too.

While Merrigan agreed to meet Kade in Montecito, she hadn't said precisely when. She was waiting for information from her team that might lead her to uncover Animus' identity. When it came in, she wanted to evaluate it on her own.

She still hadn't decided whether to discuss Kade's proposal with Rivet since she couldn't predict what his reaction would be. If K19 found Calder's files, Rivet would certainly be all for sharing. However, she doubted he, or the higher-ups, would be as benevolent if she found it first. Was it hypocritical? Absolutely.

What made the difference between Kade's offer and the decision Rivet came to was that Kade was an independent contractor. He could just as easily work for MI6 as the CIA.

"Hello, Striker," she answered when she noticed another agent's name pop up on her phone.

"How are you, Fatale?" asked the man on the other end of the call, Griffin Ellis, code name Striker.

Merrigan smiled. Years ago, shortly before joining MI6, she and the CIA operative had had a short-lived, torrid affair. Two things had come of it. First, she'd earned the code name Fatale, and second, she'd gained the closest friendship of her life.

"Frustrated."

"Ah, I see," he said. "Not with the mission, though."

"Doc wants to make a deal," she told him, wondering if it was wise to broach this subject with the man who, in essence, was Kade's boss—at least for this op.

"Go on."

"That we agree to share whatever we find."

"Not uncommon," Striker muttered.

"Right, but something tells me this mission is different."

"Not so different, sweetheart."

"What have you discovered that you're willing to share with me?" she asked impatiently.

"We haven't found anyone with the Animus code name."

Merrigan murmured that MI6 hadn't yet either. She told him she'd been scouring those closest to Leech Hess, Rory Calder, even Kade, but so far, she hadn't uncovered any clues.

"There's something I believe we've all overlooked, even the man himself."

"Which man?" Merrigan asked.

"Doc Butler."

"What's that?"

"The documents his daughter found in the floor of the cabin," said Striker.

"What do you mean?"

"Find out if he knows who hid them there."

17

Kade

Kade pulled into the circular drive of the house he'd always hoped would be his permanent home. Every day he'd spent in captivity, he dreamed of returning here. Sometimes, he dreamed Quinn would be free to come and go from the first home she'd lived in.

He'd fallen in love with the Spanish Colonial Revival house the first time he saw it. The exterior was white stucco with dark brown shutters and a red tile roof. Massive palm trees stretched high above the roof line, and bright pink bougainvillea grew up the side walls of a garage big enough to hold five cars.

As he surveyed the entryway, Kade was glad Mercer had suggested they hire a landscape crew to clean up the overgrown vegetation and plant new greenery where needed. Even the urns scattered along the driveway were overflowing with vines and flowers.

Kade walked through the front door and took a deep breath in the house that had always smelled of wood to him, maybe from the massive Douglas fir beams that adorned the vaulted ceiling. He tossed a couple of logs on the grate of the fireplace and lit it. Soon, warmth would replace the chill of the uninhabited home.

He sat on one of the oversized leather sofas and stared into the flames, wishing Merrigan had come with him rather than saying she'd meet him here. That she hadn't been willing to say when she would, troubled him.

Kade stood when the app on his phone alerted him that someone was at the gate, forgetting momentarily that it controlled the security system. When he swiped the screen, an image of Quinn appeared.

"Hello," he said after hitting the voice activation button.

"Uh, hi. Can we come in?"

"Of course." He pressed another button, and the gate opened. He chuckled and shook his head. He knew weapon technology, even understood the latest espionage gadgetry, but he was just learning how much easier it was to control his home security than it had been two years ago.

Kade whistled when he walked out the front door and saw what she was driving. "Nice car," he teased.

Quinn grinned. "I've sort of taken it over. I'll return it now, though."

"You look much better driving it than I do." The truth was he'd always intended for Quinn to have the 1962 Porsche 356B T6 Twin Grille Roadster.

"I taught her to drive," said Mercer.

"Don't forget Razor taught me how to use the clutch," she added, nudging him.

"Come inside," said Kade, motioning to the front door.

"I love this house," he heard Quinn murmur when she walked past him.

Kade smiled. "Me too. I understand you were able to spend some time here."

Quinn turned around and faced him. "I hope that's okay."

"Anytime, sweetheart. I'd like you to think of this as your home." When she smiled, he was reminded again of her mother.

"When we were here, I took Quinn down to the beach and showed her where we used to surf."

"Been too long."

"I'm ready whenever you are."

"It's mighty cold in that water in January." Kade laughed. "I sound like an old man."

"That's why they make four-threes."

"What's a four-three?" asked Quinn.

"A wetsuit you can wear when the water is too cold for humans to swim in," Kade responded.

"You're right," said Mercer. "You do sound like an old man."

"Best waves are early in the morning," Kade challenged.

"Zero five hundred it is," countered Mercer.

"Make it zero seven hundred, and you've got yourself a deal."

"You're kidding, right?" Quinn asked.

Mercer put his arm around her. "You can sleep in, precious."

Kade cleared his throat.

"Sorry—" Quinn began.

"Don't be sorry. I can't tell you how happy it makes me to see you this way."

Her cheeks turned pink. "Which way is that?"

"In love."

"About that." Mercer cleared his throat. "There's something I'd like to discuss with you."

"Something *we'd* like to discuss with you," Quinn interjected.

"Now?"

"Uh, sure." Mercer walked in the direction of the kitchen. "Do you mind?"

"Mind what?"

"I left some wine when we were here last."

"By all means. Let's open it."

Mercer reappeared with a bottle of Butler Ranch Cabernet Sauvignon and three glasses.

"I'd like to make a toast," he said after he'd opened it and poured.

"Please," prompted Kade.

"To family and to friends who become family."

"What are you saying?" Kade asked, winking at Quinn, who then turned her back to them and pulled something out of her pocket.

She turned back around and held her hand out for Kade to see. "Mercer proposed, and I said yes."

"*Wow!* That's some ring."

"It belonged to my mother," Mercer said proudly.

"It's beautiful," he said, taking a closer look at the diamond that had to be at least three karats. "As beautiful as you are, Quinn."

"Thank you." She blushed and looked between him and Mercer.

"If you're waiting for my approval, you've got it in spades."

"How did you know Mercer and I would…that he would…?"

"That I could trust Mercer with your life?"

She smiled and nodded.

"I can't answer that, but I did. I never doubted for a minute that he'd keep you safe. I guess somewhere deep in my subconscious, I also believed he'd love you."

Kade's phone buzzed, indicating someone else was at the gate. He hadn't expected Merrigan to show up this soon, but he certainly wouldn't complain that she had. He swiped the screen and saw Lena's image instead.

"Did you know she was coming?" he asked before activating the voice feature.

"Who?"

"Your mother."

"Definitely not."

"I see." Kade pressed the mic button. "Hello, Lena. This is a surprise."

"Are you going to let me in?"

"Sure." Kade pressed another button, which opened the gate, then closed the app.

"Do you want me to talk to her?" Quinn asked.

Kade shook his head, winking at her again. "Let's continue our celebration and address *boundaries* later."

Kade knew Lena well enough to read her discomfort. Was it because she was here uninvited, or was there something else going on? He'd been perfectly clear about not wanting her spending time here, and yet, here she was and had been for the past two hours. She wouldn't be staying much longer, however.

"Shit," he murmured when the app on his phone alerted him that someone else was at the gate. "Who now?" he grumbled, swiping the screen with his finger.

"Merrigan?" he said, looking at her beautiful face smiling at him.

"Surprise! I'm here."

Kade remembered to press the button to open the gate before she asked. "Come in," he said, wishing the happiness he felt at seeing her wasn't marred by Lena's presence. Dammit—why hadn't he asked her to leave fifteen minutes ago?

"Who is it?" asked Quinn.

"Merrigan is here," he told her, catching Lena's smirk out of the corner of his eye before he walked out and slammed the front door closed behind him.

"Hi," she said, climbing out of the car and walking into his arms.

"I'm so glad you're here." He wrapped his arms around her and pulled her flush against him.

"Who's here?" she asked, noticing the other two cars parked in the circular drive.

"Mercer and Quinn arrived this morning. And Lena arrived uninvited a couple of hours ago."

"I see."

"She was just leaving."

"That isn't necessary. I can—"

Before she could say another word, Kade kissed her. When her lips opened, he slid his tongue inside. He didn't care who saw them as he pushed her up against the car and ground his body into hers. That she'd shown up today made him so damn happy that even Lena being here couldn't spoil it.

He pulled back and looked into her eyes. "Like I said, she's leaving, and you're not."

"I don't want to intrude, Kade. I showed up unannounced. I know you didn't expect me today."

"You're right, but that didn't stop me from wishing you were here every minute since I arrived."

"Really?"

"Literally."

When Merrigan smiled, he felt her warmth engulf him. Everything felt right as long as she was next to him. He wished he had the words to tell her so. There were only three that came to mind, but now wasn't the time for him to say them. Later, when they were alone, he'd tell her exactly how he felt.

He took her hand in his. "Come inside."

"I, uh, brought a bag."

"Oh, darlin'," he said, picking her up and turning around and around with her in his arms. "I can't tell you how happy that makes me."

She wriggled her body against his. "I think I have a general idea."

"God, I want to be alone with you," he whispered. "Soon. Very, very soon, I will be."

"What about—"

"She's leaving."

Merrigan giggled. "I was going to say what about Quinn and Mercer?"

He grinned. "They have their own bedroom."

Kade didn't miss the daggers Lena hurled in Merrigan's direction. They couldn't have been more powerful if they'd come from her hand rather than her eyes.

"We didn't expect you," she said, walking over to where Merrigan stood beside him.

When he groaned, she squeezed his hand.

"Mom," Quinn warned.

"As I was saying, you're leaving." Kade leveled his gaze as if to challenge her to contradict him.

"Actually, I wasn't. I thought we had an engagement celebration planned."

"We'll celebrate another time," said Mercer. "I'll escort you out." He was walking toward her as he spoke, and now stood directly in front of her.

Quinn did the same and stood at Mercer's side. "Come on, Mom. I'll walk you out, then we can make plans to get together later in the week."

Kade recognized Lena's defeated expression, but he'd learned long ago not to fall victim to it.

"Sorry about that," Kade murmured when Quinn and her mother walked out the front door and closed it behind them.

"Don't be. This type of situation lends itself to discomfort."

Kade studied her. She didn't appear upset, and from his experience, she generally wasn't one to mask her feelings, intentionally or otherwise.

"Engagement celebration?" she asked.

"Yes," said Kade, happy she directed the conversation away from his ex-wife. "Looks like you'll soon be my son-in-law," he said, slapping Mercer on the back.

"I do hope I'm not intruding," she said again.

"Never." He wrapped his arm around her waist and brought her close to him. "How about a tour?"

"Sure, but is there another way out?"

Kade laughed. "We'll tour the inside first."

While Kade's blood was boiling over Lena's bullshit, he did his best to stifle it and let himself bask in the warmth of Merrigan's ethereal aura. It was as though, each time he was with her, he could physically feel hope for his future in a way he'd never thought possible.

"What are you thinking?" she asked, smiling.

"You. Always you."

Her cheeks pinkened. "You flatter me."

"It's the truth."

Kade stopped in the middle of the house's gourmet kitchen and pulled her body flush with his. He kissed her in a way he hoped conveyed the depth of his feelings.

"I'd take you to see the upstairs, but I won't want to come back down."

"Me either."

Kade hugged her tighter. "I wish you wouldn't have said that."

"Come on," said Merrigan, taking his hand. "Show me the rest of the *downstairs*."

Mercer had made an early dinner reservation at the Stonehouse at San Ysidro Ranch. "The grounds are so beautiful," he said, explaining the reason for the hour.

Once there, Kade realized he had a particular reason for wanting Quinn to see it.

"We'll be inside, enjoying a glass of wine," Kade said, letting Mercer and Quinn linger in the gardens, unhurried.

"It would be a beautiful spot for a wedding," Merrigan commented.

"I was thinking the same thing." Not just for Quinn and Mercer, but maybe for him and Merrigan someday. The thought made him smile.

"Hungry?" he asked, attempting to change the subject.

"Yes and no." She winked.

"I know what you mean."

While he hated shifting the conversation to work, he wanted her to know what had transpired since they talked about sharing information. "I have something I want to run by you," he began.

She set her glass on the bar and turned to face him. "Go ahead."

"Quinn stumbled on some documents that were hidden in the floorboards of an old cabin on Leech's property. Most of what she found belonged to me; however, I wasn't the person who hid them there."

"Funny you should bring this up."

"Why's that?"

"I spoke with Striker, earlier today, and he suggested I ask if you knew who hid them there."

"Striker? How is the old bastard?"

"First of all, as you well know, he's fine, and secondly, he's hardly old. If I recall correctly, he's your age."

"And if I recall correctly, you two had a thing for each other at one time. Should I be concerned?"

"No more so than I in regard to your ex-wife."

"Touché." Kade smiled. "Then, I have nothing to worry about. Although I am curious why you and he were discussing the case."

"Perhaps you should ask him."

"I certainly will." He smiled. They both knew full well that Striker was Kade's main contact at the agency. "Was there anything else you discussed I should be aware of?"

"Mainly that no one has been able to identify Animus."

"Interesting."

Merrigan shook her head and laughed. "What does that mean?"

"I might have a theory."

"Do you intend to tell me?"

"I have a question to ask first."

Merrigan glared at him. "Yes?"

"Have you discussed my proposal with Rivet?"

"You're a bloody bastard," she answered. "So, the premise is that if we agree to share whatever we find, you'll tell me who you think Animus is?"

"That's right."

"Shouldn't you check with Striker first?"

Kade shook his head. "I'm a lone wolf, darlin'."

Merrigan chuckled. "Oh, really? And what would your partners think if they heard you call yourself that?"

"What's that?" asked Mercer, approaching with Quinn on his arm.

"I just told Merrigan I'm a lone wolf."

He shrugged. "We all are."

18

Merrigan

Could it really be almost eight o'clock? Merrigan couldn't believe they'd sat and chatted in the Stonehouse's dining room for almost three hours. She looked about the room, thankful there were several other parties still eating.

She'd given some thought to Kade's proposal and to Striker saying it wasn't uncommon for the two agencies to cooperate.

Maybe she was overthinking it. Was her hesitation to contact Rivet driven by her contrition over her affair with Kade?

Affair? The word didn't seem to fit the way she felt about him or where she saw their relationship heading. This was nothing like any of her other romantic liaisons. Maybe that was what was behind her feelings of guilt, but what they had was hardly *illicit.*

"We want to make our home here," she heard Quinn say to Kade, realizing she hadn't been paying attention to the conversation they were having.

"It's a great idea. By here, what do you mean exactly? The Central Coast? Montecito?" Kade asked.

Mercer spoke up. "There's another offer on the table."

"And that is?"

Merrigan inwardly grinned at Kade's impatience. Couldn't the man take a breath between hearing what someone was saying to him and prodding them for the rest of the information? It wasn't that it bothered her as much as it was simply part of who he was.

While she'd be the first to agree that a relationship between operatives should be off-limits, Merrigan wondered how she could be involved with anyone but. As it was, the strength of her personality, coupled with her MI6 status, intimidated even seasoned professionals.

That would never be the case with Kade, though. The man oozed *badassery* as much as mastery. She'd never met another person, let alone a man, who made her consider relinquishing some of the control she held so close.

"My grandfather offered us the balance of the estate," Merrigan heard Quinn say.

"We would build," Mercer added.

Kade didn't answer right away, but he was skilled at masking his thoughts. Merrigan wondered if his lack of response had anything to do with the ongoing search for Calder's files, although she would think Mercer would have the same concern.

"I told my grandfather that, even though I didn't spend much time there when I was growing up, the estate still felt like home to me. That was when he said the land was ours if we wanted it."

Rather than continuing to feel like an interloper, Merrigan excused herself, hoping that by the time she returned from the ladies' room, the conversation would have moved on. However, she couldn't help wondering what Quinn's mother thought about Leech's bequest.

When she returned to the table, Kade stood and pulled her chair out, leaning in as she was seated. "Are you about ready to get out of here?"

"Yes," she murmured, feeling heat radiate from his body to hers.

Since her Jaguar and the Porsche were essentially two-seater cars, they'd driven separately, so excusing themselves and giving Mercer and Quinn time alone wasn't at all awkward.

"We'll see you in the morning?" she heard Kade ask as they said good night.

"Is it okay if we stay at the house?" Quinn asked.

"If I recall correctly, Eighty-eight and I have an appointment with the Pacific Ocean at zero seven hundred." Kade caught Merrigan's eye. "However, you and Quinn can sleep as late as you'd like."

When the valet brought the car around, Merrigan went directly to the passenger door, hoping Kade wouldn't mind.

"I was going to ask if I could drive," he said, winking.

She rested her head against the seat and let the pleasantries of their evening wash over her. It had been a long time since she'd sat around a dinner table, talking for as long as they had, and even longer since she'd spent any time whatsoever with what was left of her family.

Her parents had passed away ten years ago, within two months of each other. Her only other immediate relative was an older brother she wasn't close to. She supposed it was one reason why long missions never bothered her. What else would she have done with her time if she wasn't working? Certainly not spend it with her brother, his wife, and their children, since they'd never invited her to.

Admittedly, she'd enjoyed talking with Quinn about their wedding plans, although she had nothing to offer based on her own experience. The only thing she'd added, that she thought Quinn might find useful, was that their wishes for their marriage ceremony should be all that mattered.

Years ago, she'd been a bridesmaid and had witnessed one of her dearest friend's day nearly ruined by the interference of her own mother and the groom's. She vowed that, if she ever were to marry—as unlikely as that would be—all she would want in attendance would be her, her future husband, and whoever was marrying them.

She glanced at Kade, who was studying her while he waited for the stoplight to turn from red to green.

"I wish I could read your thoughts," he murmured, stroking his finger down her cheek.

"I'm happy to share. I was thinking about how nice tonight was and how I don't remember another like it."

"Me either. Quinn is…"

Merrigan waited for him to finish, and when he didn't, she offered her opinion. "Remarkable."

"Isn't she?"

"Given her upbringing, she is spectacular."

"I like that word too." Kade looked away from her. "I'm so proud of her."

His voice had changed, and so had the look on his face.

"Now, I wish I could read your thoughts."

"I'll explain when we get back to the house."

The rest of the ride was quiet until they got to the gate. While they waited for it to open, Kade's phone vibrated. By the time he pulled into the drive, Merrigan's phone began to ping as well.

"Leech. What can I do for you?" she asked.

"Do you know where Doc is?"

His tone worried her. "I'm with him. Why? What's wrong?"

"It's Lena," he said with a shaky voice. "There's been an accident."

"I'll let you talk to him directly," she said, handing the phone to Kade. "It's Leech."

She overheard him explain Lena's car had gone off the road not too far from his place. Paps was the one who had alerted both emergency vehicles as well as her father when he grew concerned that her tracking device hadn't indicated movement, although it was continually updating.

"She's in intensive care at the hospital in Santa Barbara," Leech said.

"Are you with her?" Kade asked.

"On my way. Paps and Razor are with me."

"I'm ten minutes away. I'll meet you there." He ended the call and turned to her. "I'm sorry."

"Please, Kade. Don't be."

"Do you want to stay here or come with me?"

"Which would you prefer?" she asked.

"It may be a long night."

"Understood. I'll be here if you need anything."

Kade got out of the car and climbed into his father's truck. "I'll keep you posted," he said.

"What about Quinn?" she asked.

"Can you call Eighty-eight?"

"Of course."

Kade was beyond the gate before Merrigan realized she had no way to get into the house, and after witnessing the intricacies of the security system, she knew there'd be no sneaking in. Instead, she got behind the wheel of her car and placed the call to Mercer.

After alerting him of Lena's accident, she started the engine, pulled through the gates that opened automatically when she approached, and drove to her rental house in Cayucos. When she heard from Kade, she'd simply explain she hadn't been able to get in and didn't want to waylay him from getting to the hospital.

The forethought explanation wasn't needed, though, because twenty-four hours later, she still hadn't heard from him.

19

Merrigan

They weren't any closer to discovering Animus' identity than they had been three weeks ago. Merrigan wondered whether Kade had been telling her the truth when he said he had a theory about who it might be, given when she'd asked Razor about the conversation, he informed her Kade hadn't mentioned it to him.

Merrigan doubted that was the truth, but her entire relationship with Kade—Doc, as she reminded herself to think of him—was based solely on the lies they told each other.

She'd been the first to tell him a mistruth when she said she understood why he had to spend every day at the hospital with Quinn and her mother.

What little news she received came from Razor, and he'd informed her Lena's condition had initially been critical and remained serious.

She refrained from asking why Doc had taken it upon himself to become her primary medical advocate.

"What's going on with Paps?" she asked. It seemed as though he'd disappeared.

"He's taken a step back," Razor responded.

"What does that mean?"

"He's at the hospital daily, but steers clear of Doc and Quinn. Most likely, he's found someone willing to update him on Barbie's progress so he doesn't have to ask them."

"I don't understand."

"It's a guess on my part, but my belief is that, somewhere along the way, Paps fell hard for the woman he claimed to detest. Now, who knows if she even remembers him." Razor shrugged. "Like I said, I'm hypothesizing."

Merrigan checked her watch. She'd have to leave soon for a meeting she'd scheduled with Striker. Since Doc was no longer involved, at least for the time being, they'd agreed to work together on finding Animus and only consult with K19 when necessary.

"Where are you off to?" Razor asked when she put her laptop in its case.

She'd taken to working in Harmony, given the K19 team had set up a state-of-the-art intelligence operation in the small house.

"I have a meeting in Los Angeles this evening. I won't be back until tomorrow at the earliest."

"With Boris?"

Merrigan laughed. "Striker."

"Same thing, Natasha. He's the one who gave you the code name, right?"

"Watch out, or I'll start calling you Rocky."

"Wait. Not Bullwinkle?"

"I'd think you'd prefer Rocky, given it's short for Rocket. Besides, Paps is more of a Bullwinkle."

The look on Razor's face changed so drastically that she thought perhaps she'd insulted him.

"That's what makes him so deadly. Everyone underestimates Paps."

"I didn't mean—"

"I know you didn't. He's been my best friend for close to twenty-five years, and he won't even talk to me about what he's going through."

"Have you considered discussing it with Doc?"

Razor shook his head and looked away.

She knew enough about LA traffic to expect to be sitting bumper-to-bumper, given her later-than-expected start. However, she was almost to Westwood, and so far, it had been an easy drive.

Merrigan used the voice-activation system built into the car to request a call be placed to "Griffin" since the computerized assistant consistently failed to locate Striker in her contact list.

"Where are you?" he asked.

"Beyond the Getty."

"You're kidding. Did you fly partway?"

She laughed. "I'm as shocked as you by the lack of traffic."

"Where are you staying?"

"Hotel Bel-Air."

"Damn. I was hoping you'd say the Robmar."

"It was booked."

Striker laughed like she had. "Too rich for us, mere governmental employees, anyway. To stay in digs like that, you'd have to be on K19's payroll."

He was joking, but Merrigan couldn't bring herself to laugh.

"You still there?"

"Yes. Sorry."

"I'm at the Bel-Air too. I'll meet you in the lobby with a Bramble in hand."

"That sounds brilliant."

"Let Striker take care of you tonight, Fatale."

Merrigan ended the call, wondering what he'd meant. Certainly not in a romantic way, right? They'd been friends for so long that crying on his shoulder when necessary had become second-nature, but only because she saw him as a substitute for her own big brother. If he wanted something different, it would devastate her because she certainly didn't.

The phone buzzed at least four times during their late lunch, but Merrigan refused to look at it. She knew Rivet wasn't calling, because she had a different alert for him. It wasn't Doc either, not that she had a special alert for him; he'd just stopped contacting her.

"Answer it," prodded Striker.

"No. Whatever it is can wait."

He reached across the table and took her hand in his. "I've never seen you so tightly wound, and I've seen you in plenty of life-threatening situations. What's going on? Is it Doc?"

"No," she snapped. "Okay, well, yes. Maybe. I don't know."

"Talk to me, Fatale."

She took a drink of the second or third Bramble he'd ordered for her; she'd lost count, and since she wasn't driving, she didn't care how many she had.

"We can sit here all afternoon and evening if you'd like. Eventually, you'll get *pished* enough to talk."

"All right, what the hell? Remember, later, when you're bloody well ready to wring my neck, that you asked for this."

She let loose and told him everything that had happened. She started with how Doc had left her in the driveway with no way to get into his house, then didn't contact her for close to forty-eight hours.

Every text and phone call they'd had since, she reported in minute detail. She told him how she'd driven to the hospital *twice,* intending to see him, but left without going inside. And then, finally, she told Striker she'd gone and let herself fall in love with the bastard who'd probably forgotten all about her.

"Whew," he said. "That was quite a story. Feel better now?"

"Not the slightest."

"You need to get laid, sweetheart, and in a hurry."

"Griff, I—"

"Not by me. That wouldn't do you any good at all. *By him.*"

"What are you suggesting? That I prance into the hospital and drag him to the nearest supply closet?" She groaned. Of course that reminded her of when they were in Ramstein and he'd asked if she'd seen one.

"She's been released."

"How do you…never mind. That was a stupid question."

He studied her.

"I can't."

"Sure, you can. Start by calling him. Tell him you heard Lena was well enough to be released and that you…uh…how should I put this? You *miss* him."

"I *miss* him?"

"It's a euphemism."

Merrigan finished what was left of her drink, then rested her elbow on the table and her chin in her hand. "Why couldn't I have fallen in love with you?"

"You know why not."

She sat up straight. "I *don't*. Tell me."

"You would've chewed me up and spit me out if I'd given you the chance. There's only one man who I believe can hold your interest long enough that it might just last forever."

Obviously, he meant Doc since she'd just confessed to being in love with him. "What if he's already spit me out?"

"Not a chance. Just look at you."

She smiled. Right now, she probably looked like a haggard, drunken mess. At least that's how she felt.

"You're beautiful, Fatale. The hardest thing I ever did was let you go, but I knew I had to."

"Griffin…"

"Here's what we're going to do. I'm going to escort you to your room, give you a very chaste kiss on the cheek, make sure you lock the door once you're inside, and slink off to my room. You're going to call Doc Butler and tell him it's time he paid attention to you instead of his ex-wife."

She definitely wouldn't be telling him that, but maybe she would call him. She longed to hear his voice, and she was just drunk enough that she might not talk herself out of it.

"Maybe…"

"That's my girl. Actually, you're not. You're his girl. *Damn,* I envy that man."

"You don't mean it," she murmured.

"You have no idea how much I do. Come on. Let's go before I change my mind and keep you all to myself, even though I know you'd be miserable," he muttered.

Merrigan opened the bottle of water she'd left on the table next to the bed, took a drink, and stared at her phone. She'd been wrong earlier when she didn't check her cell because she assumed it wasn't Kade calling. It had been, and he'd left several messages saying, first, that he needed to talk to her and, finally, that he had to see her as soon as possible.

A few minutes ago, she'd been determined to call him. Now, she wasn't sure. What was with the sudden urgency? Did he, like Striker had said about her, need to get laid too?

She scrolled through her history to see when he'd last called before today and wasn't surprised to see it had been two days ago. The length of the call was even more troubling; they'd only talked for four minutes.

She rolled over and hugged her pillow. *Why* in the bloody hell had she let herself fall in love with him?

There was only one other time in her life when she'd thought she was in love, and it had almost destroyed her. She met the man who'd captured her heart in much the same way she'd met Kade, although she hadn't rescued Sergei Orlov; it had been the other way around. Or it had appeared that way to her at the time.

When that affair ended, she'd vowed never to allow herself to fall for another agent—CIA, FSB, or even MI6. There was a reason it was frowned upon in her line of work, and she'd come close to losing everything because she hadn't followed the rules.

With that reminder, she set the phone on the table beside her.

Merrigan had drifted off with the television and bedside light still on. At first, she thought she was dreaming when she heard a knock at the door, or maybe it was on the telly, but when she heard it again, louder than before, she got up to see who it was.

She looked through the peephole, stunned to see Doc on the other side.

"Hi," she said, releasing the door chain so she could open it all the way. "What are you doing here?"

"You wouldn't answer my calls."

"How did you know where…never mind. Striker told you."

Doc nodded, closed the door, and put his arm around her waist. "We need to talk, but first, I have to do this." Kade kissed her, then lifted her in his arms and carried her to the bed.

"Doc, we—"

He kissed her again, harder, and wove his fingers in her hair.

"Wait," she said, rolling out from under him.

"You're right," he said, scrubbing his face with his hand. "I need to tell you why I'm here."

Merrigan sat up and rested against the headboard.

Doc sat on the edge of the other side of the bed and leaned over to untie his boots. "I'm taking them off," he said over his shoulder.

"Good. No boots on the bed. It's bad luck."

"I thought it was bad luck to put a hat on the bed."

"Oh, you might be right. No boots on the bed anyway."

When she smiled, he couldn't stop looking at her.

"What?"

"I love your smile."

"You flatter me, Doc."

"The name's Kade, Fatale." He scooted up so he was sitting next to her, reached over, and held her hand.

"How is Lena?" she asked.

"Progressing. It seems as though some of her memory is returning. Today when we arrived at the house, she said something about how she'd always loved the bougainvillea."

"She's at the house?"

"Yes." Doc scrubbed his face for the second time. "I should've started there. She was released from the hospital earlier today, and we brought her to the house to continue her recovery."

"I see."

"Quinn and Mercer are living there for now, and we hired a nurse." Kade's expression changed.

"What?"

He shook his head, turned to his side, and put his arm around her waist. "I've missed you so much."

She'd tell him she'd missed him too, but she wasn't the one who'd gone MIA for the past month.

"It's nice of you to let her stay with you."

"When the doctors said she could go home if we could afford to hire medical help, I made the decision without thinking it through."

His expression changed again.

"What aren't you saying?" she asked.

"I'll get to that later. First, I want to hear about you. How have you been, Fatale?"

She crossed her arms and leveled her gaze on him. "I've been *fine,* thank you."

"Okay…What I was going to say is she's overly dependent on me. I can see it already."

"You've spent a great deal of time with her."

"You're right. I have." He looked into her eyes. "You aren't saying much."

"It isn't any of my business."

"I'd make it my business if you had another man living in your house."

Merrigan shrugged. What could she say? He hadn't consulted her about the accident or anything afterwards; he'd merely given her brief updates. To ask her opinion now seemed too little, too late.

"Talk to me, Fatale. What are you thinking?"

"Tell me why she's really there, Doc."

"The name's Kade," he repeated, getting up from the bed. "Can I get you something to drink?" he asked.

"Soda with lime please," she answered, pointing to a credenza.

"Do they restock this every day?"

She figured he was referring to the wide selection of booze and mixers along with fresh limes, lemons, and oranges in the chiller. She nodded and took the glass he handed to her.

He poured himself a Scotch, also neat, and sat on the bed with his back to her.

"Whatever it is, say it, Doc."

"There are two sides to what I'm about to tell you. The first is why she's at Casa Carrizo. The second, well, I'll get to that."

"Go on."

"I never really loved her, not even all those years ago," he began. "At first, I thought I did, but once I heard I'd been accepted into the NCS, I was more than ready to leave everything behind, including Lena."

"You married her."

"Because of Quinn." He thought for a minute. "That isn't true. I stayed with her as long as I did because of our daughter. Initially, I married her out of guilt."

"Kade." She sighed. She could no longer consider him Doc. Not when he was baring his soul to her.

"It was my fault Calder raped her."

"It wasn't, and you know it. Calder was a greedy, narcissistic sociopath."

"Leech told me to go out that night. He thought it would be better if I wasn't there when he told Calder he was being separated from the program we were both in. Lena felt sorry for him. It was that simple. So she went to talk to him, and no one was there to defend her."

He told her that being around Quinn so much the last three weeks had brought back memories of what her mother was like before the rape. The idea of her suffering at the hands of a monster like Calder made Kade want to kill the man all over again.

"I can't imagine the level of guilt Leech feels. He's been pushing hard for Lena and me to get back together. I'm sure it's because of his own regret." He rested his hand on hers and stroked it with his thumb. "I think that's why Elisabetta left me half the estate. It's the only logical explanation."

"Because she hoped you and Lena would be together again?"

Kade nodded. "I tell myself I tried to make the marriage work, but I didn't. I hid behind the work I did."

He told her about the day he realized they had to divorce. "I was kept in a cage as part of a training exercise. I had to stay in there for twenty-four hours with no food and very little hydration." Not all of the trainees made it the entire time, but Kade told her he hadn't had any trouble at all. "Every time I thought I couldn't stand another minute, I thought about Lena and how I'd rather be kept in the cage for a month rather than spend the same amount of time with her."

Merrigan gasped. "I'm sorry. I didn't mean to do that. Please, go on."

"It makes me the biggest asshole you've ever known, right?"

She shook her head. "I can't pretend I know how you felt at the time."

"Quinn had just turned five. It took me another two years to finally go through with it."

"When she went to boarding school."

Kade nodded. He'd told her about Quinn's education before, and she'd explained boarding school was more common and far better perceived in the UK.

"I feel like I'm rambling."

"Go back to my original question. Why is Lena there?"

Kade took a deep breath and blew it out slowly. "When I walked into the hospital after the accident…"

His voice caught, and he took several more deep breaths before continuing. "She looked so much like she had after Calder…"

Merrigan shifted and put her arm around him. She leaned into him so her body was pressed against his back.

"Keep talking," she whispered.

"He'd beaten her so badly that she looked like she'd been in a car accident."

He rested his hand on hers, so thankful for her touch.

"We were engaged to be married, and instead of staying with her to help her get over what Calder had done, I accepted my orders and shipped out.

"When I came back a few weeks later for Christmas, it was like she was a different person. She was afraid of everything, including me. She'd startle when I'd walk into the room, and if I tried to talk to her, she'd cower. She was so broken, and on top of everything else, she was pregnant."

"With whose child?"

Kade didn't respond directly to the question but kept talking about Lena. "I was relentless about being with her. I decided that if I was, eventually, she'd go back to being the way she was before the rape. I know now how naive that was. Anyway, it wasn't long before the scales tipped the other way. She started depending on me for everything, particularly after we got married. She didn't make a decision about even the smallest things without consulting me. Because of the rape and the pregnancy, plus me working for the NCS, we kept the marriage a secret from everyone but our parents."

"So now, you're caring for her in the same way you think you should've then?"

"Yes," he said, hanging his head.

"What happened to Calder after the rape?" she asked.

"He was arrested, but made bail almost immediately. That he couldn't leave the county while awaiting trial worked to the Russians' advantage."

In hindsight, it was obvious to Merrigan that Calder had been a prime recruit target for the Maskhadovs. He spoke the language almost fluently, his volatile temperament had been well-documented, and clearly, the Russians knew he was being released from training, and struck at the perfect time.

She knew Kade's father was the one who'd discovered someone had been hacking into Leech's system, decoding thousands of classified documents, and handing them off to the Maskhadov organization.

Consequently, many US agents had been systematically assassinated when their covers were blown.

"How long had your father been retired when all this happened?"

"Officially?"

Merrigan nodded.

"Let's see. Naughton was thirteen, so ten years."

"Do any of your siblings know how your parents met?"

Kade shook his head. "When I was around eight, I started asking questions about what Da did. He sat me down and explained why it was important I not only stop asking, but also promise never to talk about it again. It wasn't until I told him I wanted to join the Marines that he told me more about his life and career."

"You've carried the burden of secrecy since you were quite young. No wonder you're so good at it."

"Not something I'm proud of."

"It's a trait necessary to what we do," she murmured. "Tell me how you caught Calder."

"We almost didn't," said Kade. "But Leech discovered someone had been in the wine caves. The vineyard and winery weren't operational at the time, so there would be no reason for anyone to be in there."

Kade stood. "Can I get you anything else?"

She held up her still half-full glass. "I'm good."

He poured himself another drink.

"I was on stakeout three nights in a row. The first two nights, I didn't see a living soul except for a couple of coyotes. The third night, though, was when it all went down."

Kade told her he saw Calder entering the caves with another person. He called Leech, waited for him to arrive, then followed him inside.

"It was obvious Calder and his goons had been alerted he was on his way in," he said. "Leech had barely gotten inside when I followed and saw them. They both had guns leveled straight at him."

"You killed Nitko that night."

While few knew the details, the fact that a brand-new NCS agent had taken down one of Russia's most lethal assassins became legendary. With a single shot, Kade had ended Aliya "Nitko" Pavlichenko's unbroken kill record. It was the first time she'd missed and the last time she took a breath.

"I was a split second away from ending Calder when Leech stopped me."

"And he escaped."

Kade nodded and gripped the back of his neck. "There's something else I need to tell you, and I've put it off long enough." He handed her what was left of his Scotch. "You're gonna need this."

"Tell me why, Kade."

"Because Lena will probably be staying at the house indefinitely."

"For what reason?"

"Because she wasn't in an accident. She was run off the road intentionally."

Merrigan was stunned. "Why?"

"I have no idea. Every theory I've come up with doesn't lead anywhere."

"It doesn't make sense," she murmured.

Kade nodded.

"It must be somehow tied to Animus."

"I agree," he said.

"Which reminds me, you told me you thought you knew who Animus was."

"I told you I *might* have an idea."

"And?"

"The more I thought about it, the more far-fetched it seemed. Besides, it couldn't be. The person I suspected is dead."

"Have you asked yourself whom the intel on Animus came from? I haven't been able to get a read on it from either Striker or Rivet. It's like it just appeared."

"That bothers me as well. If it hadn't come through my father, I'd say it was amateurish."

She walked over to the desk and powered up her laptop.

"What are you doing?" he asked.

"Making arrangements to leave the States."

He joined her and closed her computer. "Fatale…" he murmured, drawing her body closer to his. He bent down to kiss her, and when she kissed him back, he picked her up and carried her to the bed.

He kissed down the side of her neck. "I can't stand the idea of being away from you again."

"Kade…"

"I want you, Merrigan. More than that, I need you."

She wanted him too, but was this a good idea? Even if it wasn't, could she resist him?

20

Kade

Merrigan's eyes bored into his as he watched her unbutton her blouse and shimmy out of it. Before she could unfasten her bra, he was on her.

"Too slow," he muttered, finishing what she'd started until she stood before him naked. "On the bed," he demanded.

She sat on the edge, and he pushed her back, covering her breasts with his hands and her body with his. When he teased her nipples with his fingers and his mouth, Merrigan writhed beneath him.

Kade shifted off her, stood, and pulled his shirt over his head, then unfastened his belt. He stood before her naked like she had him.

She looked him up and down.

"Like what you see?" he asked.

"Very much," she answered.

"Me too."

He was on her again, opening her thighs with his knee. He positioned himself near her sex, but stopped and looked into her eyes. "Merrigan, I…"

"Don't talk. Just make love to me."

He did as she asked with a groan that matched hers.

Her lips parted the moment his tongue touched them, and he swooped in. Her body spasmed and clenched around him as the first orgasm consumed her.

He slowed while she drifted back to earth, but as soon as she had, he thrust into her again, his hands digging into her hips. He stopped then, but only long enough to flip her over before he resumed pounding her from behind.

"Give me another one, Fatale. One more," he urged.

A few more thrusts, coupled with the attention he gave her clit, sent her soaring. This time, he joined her, growling out his release.

"That's more like it." He moaned, pulling her with him as he sank into the bed. When she tried to squirm away, he held her close. "Stay still, Fatale. We aren't anywhere near finished yet."

"I don't think I can…"

"But you will," he murmured. His hands moved over the front of her body—one on her breast, the other between her legs as he brought her spent nerves back to life. He snuggled into her and nibbled her shoulder as his fingers toyed with her sex. She gasped and clung to him as a third powerful orgasm caught her off guard.

She tried again to wriggle away from him, but he wouldn't give her reprieve. He pushed her back on the bed and covered her with his body. She could feel his hardness resting against her.

"You'll break me." She moaned.

"Don't you worry, Fatale," he said, thrusting into her again. "I'll put you back together."

He'd lost track of how many times he wrung pleasure from her before he finally moved away from her. She let her eyes drift closed, but he wasn't ready to let her sleep. He went into the bathroom and ran water in the tub big enough for both of them, then returned to where she slept and swept her in his arms.

He carried her into the bathroom and gently set her in the warm water. Once he was seated behind her, he turned on the jets, and she moaned.

He ran his hands up and down her arms while his lips made their way across her back and up the side of her neck. "From the very first time I heard your voice, I was sure you were an angel. You have to be. No mere human can be as perfect as you," he murmured.

With one hand he swept her hair away, running his tongue from her neck back down to her shoulder. She shuddered when he nipped at her sensitive skin.

There was so much more Kade needed to say. He wanted to tell her that he hadn't known what true love felt like until he met her. He wanted her to know he intended to spend the rest of his life worshiping her body with his, like he just had. If she'd let him, he'd promise to never let a day go by without bringing her the pleasure he knew only he could wring from her.

He wanted to spend hours talking to her, like the moments they'd stolen when he was being held prisoner. She didn't just listen to him; she told him her life stories too.

He'd tell her he longed to be by her side as she showed him the places he'd only been able to picture in his imagination. And her descriptions of the Scottish moors had been so vivid he could almost feel the chill of the moist air.

He'd tell her he wanted to travel again to all the places he'd only seen garbed in tactical gear, gun in hand. And that they could eat, drink, and make love their way around the globe, knowing they'd left the danger of their previous lives behind and were free to love each other without fear of the future.

He wanted her to know that no one could be more perfect for him than she was, and he for her. That they each understood the lives the other had lived until now, and when the horrors of those lives crept into their nightmares, like they always did, they could comfort each other in a way no one else would be able to.

He realized, in that moment, he could walk away from Casa Carrizo and let Lena live the rest of her life there if she needed to. It wouldn't matter where he and Merrigan lived. No walls could ever mean as much to him as having her wrapped in his arms or his body sunk deep into hers.

He was truly in love for the first time in his life, and he would never let go of this feeling, or of her. This was why he'd endured the pain the Russians inflicted on his body; this was why he'd never given up. Little did he know then that heaven was right there with him. His angel had carried him through the darkness into a light he never knew existed.

But somehow, he knew he couldn't tell her any of these things, not yet anyway. She wasn't as ready to hear them as he was to say them. So, he'd keep them to himself until the day he knew she'd be ready to listen and to answer.

For now, he'd show her how he felt in every way he could think of.

21

Merrigan

Every muscle in her body ached from the most intense night of lovemaking she'd ever experienced. Kade had been relentless in coaxing orgasm after orgasm out of her. So much so that when they finally slept, she didn't have the energy to even dream.

She rolled to her side and took in the sight of the beautiful man still asleep next to her. As much as she longed to run her finger over the scar that went from under his left ear, across his cheek, and down to his chin, she wouldn't, nor would she ever ask how he got it.

Merrigan knew well enough that some wounds were too painful to relive by telling their story. However it had happened, didn't matter. He'd lived through it. That was the important part.

She had one of those scars too. It ran from her throat, down her sternum, and under her left breast. She should've died that day. It was only by the grace of God that she hadn't bled out.

He hadn't asked her about it, and he wouldn't. It was an unspoken rule between people in their profession. It was the same with kills. No one asked, because they all knew—one was too many.

Kade moaned, his left arm twitched, and his brow furrowed. She waited a few seconds, but when he grew more agitated, Merrigan got out of bed and nudged it with her leg.

"Kade, wake up," she said in a gentle but loud enough voice to break through his nightmare. She nudged the bed a second time, a little harder, and he opened his eyes. It took a few seconds for him to register where he was, and in that time, she got back into bed.

"I'm sorry."

"Don't be," she soothed, wrapping her arm around his waist and resting her head on his chest. "It happens to the best of us."

"It happens more when I'm overly tired." He grinned, which made her smile.

"Can you go back to sleep?"

He reached over her to the nightstand, where he'd left his watch. "It's after ten."

With the blackout drapery in the hotel room, it was hard to tell whether it was day or night. When she woke a little while ago, she hadn't bothered to check the time.

"I'm awake. What about you?" he asked.

"I'm hungry."

With his arm still around her waist, Kade rolled her to her side, so she was facing him.

"I know you have to leave, and I sure as hell wish I could go with you. Lena…" he said.

"I know."

"I'm not sure how to handle the situation I've put myself in."

"I have no experience with this kind of thing, Kade."

He sighed. "I don't know many people who do."

"Tell me the specifics of her condition."

Kade told her Lena's memory seemed to be returning little by little, but her eyesight hadn't. His biggest worry was that it never would.

"When I saw her coming through security at the airport, the morning we left for Germany to see Leech, I almost didn't recognize her. She looked younger than she had in years. It was as though when the heavy burden of stress was finally lifted with Calder's death, her body had shed its armor. Quinn noticed it too. Neither of us could believe how different she looked."

Merrigan couldn't help but feel sorry for the woman. She'd finally gotten her life back only to have another tragedy strike. "She's gone from being imprisoned by the threat of danger, to being imprisoned by her injuries," she murmured, not necessarily meaning to say it out loud.

Kade nodded in agreement. "And the threat of danger has returned."

"You should be there, Kade."

He sighed. "Not yet. I have no idea when I might see you again."

The flight from Los Angeles to Heathrow would take ten hours, after which, Merrigan had a meeting scheduled with Rivet. When that ended, she'd return to the airport, where she'd catch another flight to Glasgow. Travel and meeting time, all together, would be sixteen grueling hours. Even then, she wouldn't be at her final destination.

She settled into her first-class seat, turned off her phone, and looked out the window, already missing Kade.

The goodbye she said to him this morning had been the most difficult of her life, mainly because she rarely said it. The last time she had was when they'd parted ways in Moscow after his and Leech's escape from the Maskhadovs. Before that? She didn't even remember saying goodbye to anyone in her family.

He'd made it more difficult by giving her a gift this morning. That he'd stayed with her another day and night was the best present she could've asked for, but he hadn't stopped there.

This morning, while they were still side by side in bed and naked, he'd told her to close her eyes. She felt him fasten something around her neck and waited patiently for him to tell her she could look.

"Open," he'd said, and while she couldn't see the necklace, she'd traced the heart-shaped piece with her fingers.

"It's a family heirloom. Happy Valentine's Day."

"I didn't realize…" It wasn't a holiday that ever registered on Merrigan's radar.

"It's okay. I wanted to give this to you before you left; the holiday is just another reason to."

When he finally let her get up and look in the mirror, tears had come to her eyes. The locket had a red ruby background with a vine of gold and diamond flowers.

"Look inside," he'd said.

When she had, she saw not only a photo of herself she didn't remember having taken, but one of him too.

"In my heart, we're together, Fatale. And now, we are in yours too."

When they spoke right before she boarded the plane, he told her Quinn reported her mother had had a couple of bad days and had asked for him repeatedly. That his daughter hadn't contacted him spoke volumes about how she felt about her mother's dependence on him.

Merrigan's morning call to Rivet had been brief. He was already aware of the circumstances surrounding Lena's accident and had been anticipating not only her call, but her impending arrival.

Knowing it would be ten hours before she could check her cell phone again, Merrigan powered it up one last time. Instead of a call or message from Kade, there were both from Striker.

"I only have a few minutes before my flight leaves," she said when he picked up after the first ring.

"Your flight where?"

"You know I can't answer that."

"So the Hotel Bel-Air reunion didn't go as well as I'd hoped?"

"No, it did. We had hours of mind-blowing sex before saying goodbye."

"At least you got laid."

"Yeah, well. I'm due again. But listen, I've got to go. The cabin guard is giving me the evil eye."

"Cabin guard?"

"She lit into me when I called her a stewardess. I guess it's no longer PC."

"Hasn't been for about thirty years, sweetheart. Now, tell me quick. Where are you going?"

Merrigan disconnected the call without answering. That Striker had asked twice bothered her immensely, particularly after she'd told him the first time that she couldn't say.

Presently, Kade was the only person who knew where she was headed. Once she briefed Rivet, he would be the second. Otherwise, no one else would be able to locate her.

It was more than ten years since she'd set foot in the town she grew up in. The last was for her father's funeral, only two months after her mother's.

There had been a time in her life when she vowed never to return, but that was when she was young, determined to see the world, and tired of the tiny hamlet. Now, she craved visiting the simple place where nothing much ever changed.

Seeing Kade with his family had also left her yearning for a connection with her own. Once she arrived, she'd contact her brother.

She felt her seat vibrate and realized she'd put her phone in the side pocket but hadn't turned it off. When she pulled it out to do so, she couldn't help but notice there was another text, from Kade. She laughed when she saw the message consisted of two emojis. The first was a broken heart and the second, a crying face. That a big, burly, tough-as-nails, badass ex-CIA agent sent her such a message made her smile.

22

Kade

There was a message from Maddox on his phone but nothing from Merrigan. He hadn't expected there to be, but he was still disappointed.

"What do you need, Mad?" he snapped when his brother answered his call.

"*Whoa.* What's goin' on?"

There was no simple answer. He was overwhelmed by things he couldn't control. Between Merrigan leaving, the unpredictability of Lena's condition, and the renewed threat of danger, his blood pressure was skyrocketing.

"Sorry," he muttered.

"Alex told me to call and invite you and Merrigan to dinner at Stave Saturday night. She and Peyton are hosting a Valentine's shindig."

"Wish I could, brother, but Merrigan has left town."

"I see. That explains your shitty attitude. Well, sorry, bro. Maybe next year, you'll have a date. I guess you could bring—"

"Don't," Kade spat.

"Just jokin'."

"Don't do it again."

"Got a minute?" Mercer asked a few minutes later.

"Sure. What's up?"

"Let's take a ride."

They walked out the front door to the circular drive.

"We'll need to take yours since that's all I've got," said Mercer, pointing to his Ducati motorcycle.

"You mean Quinn's Porsche or my dad's old truck?" Kade laughed for the first time since he said goodbye to Merrigan, and it felt good. "We're a pair. We could probably both afford two or three cars, and we don't have any."

Mercer grinned. "The Jag is in an underground lot in New York, so you have one more car than I do."

"I've been thinking about that."

"I'll make arrangements to have it shipped here."

Mercer told him about the night Quinn first met him and how she'd found him hovering on the periphery of the party she'd attended. "That was the night I realized I shouldn't be her detail lead any longer."

"It all worked out, Eighty-eight."

They threw the surfboards into the bed, in case the waves were decent, and took the truck down to the beach.

"What did you want to talk about?" Kade asked as they walked across the sand.

"Lena."

Kade inwardly groaned.

"Something isn't right."

When they got close to the edge of the water, both men sat down.

"Elaborate," said Kade.

"I know you picked up on her comment about the bougainvillea when you brought her home from the hospital."

"The doctors did say she'd have sporadic and possibly isolated memories."

"There's been more."

"Again, I think that's to be expected."

"That same afternoon, I heard her tell the nurse you were her husband and that, while it had been several years since you and she had lived in Casa Carrizo, it was good to be home."

Kade rubbed the back of his neck. "*Were* her husband."

"Present tense, Doc."

"You don't think she was confused."

Mercer shook his head. "Not an isolated incident either, Doc. The things I've picked up on happen when she thinks no one can hear or see her."

"Are we talking surveillance, Eighty-eight?"

"Not yet, but that's the primary reason I wanted to talk to you."

"Go on."

"As you know, I had Burns oversee updating the security at Casa Carrizo."

Kade laughed. "I've had to get up to speed pretty fast. My father…Well, you know how he is."

Mercer nodded. "It's state of the art. We could surveil her without invading her, uh, personal privacy."

He shuddered and laughed. "I was married to her at one time, but honestly, I see her more like a sister now. I can't imagine…"

"Me either," said Mercer, not laughing. "So, you're good with it?"

"Do what you think is necessary, Eighty-eight."

"Thanks, Doc."

"Made any progress on the wedding plans?"

Mercer watched the waves crashing on the shore and didn't answer right away. "I think it's best we wait."

Kade understood his reasoning, but in their line of work, danger loomed behind every corner. Waiting wouldn't change anything, and postponing because of a purported threat meant the bad guys won.

"Don't," he said. "Get married; live your lives. There will come a time when you face it head on—your own mortality, that is—and when you do, don't have regrets, particularly where love is concerned."

"Sounds like you're speaking from experience."

"Not as much in the past as the present."

"Merrigan?"

Kade nodded. He and Lena never should've married. They'd done it for all the wrong reasons. And Peyton was better off with Brodie. She and his brother loved each other, and it made him happy to see them together. But Merrigan? She was different than any other woman he'd ever known. It wasn't just that it was new. He couldn't imagine anyone who was a better match for him, and he for her.

Even yesterday morning, when she woke him from a nightmare, she'd handled it perfectly. Knowing the risks involved in waking someone with PTSD, she'd nudged the bed and said his name. The two combined woke him up, but not in a way that might result in him lashing out at her unintentionally.

While she would be the first to downplay her rock-star status in the field, it was widely accepted as fact that Fatale wasn't just one of the best female agents MI6 had ever had, but one of the best agents in general. Hell, she'd saved his ass.

"What did you say earlier about Quinn? Something about realizing you shouldn't be on her detail?"

Mercer nodded.

"I've realized I shouldn't be in the game anymore, in large part thanks to Merrigan. What's more, I don't want to be."

"So quit."

"I tried." Kade laughed. "Paps wouldn't let me." Mercer knew as well as he did that he was joking. However, one thing Paps was right about was the four of them—him, Mercer, Razor, and Paps—had to decide together whether K19 stayed in business or dissolved.

"What about you, Eighty-eight?"

"I told Quinn that, as soon as this mission wrapped, I was done."

"That leaves Paps and Razor. I don't know about Paps, but what in the hell would Sharp do?"

Mercer laughed. "Who knows? Maybe he's as ready to quit as we are."

"Kade, is that you?" asked Lena.

He'd been standing just outside the door leading from the kitchen to the patio, watching her since he and Eighty-eight returned from the beach. "Mm-hmm," he muttered, not asking how she knew he was there.

"What are you doing?"

"Can I get you anything?" he asked.

She leaned forward and ran her hand along the tabletop until her fingertips touched the base of the glass of wine she'd been drinking. The display of finding her glass was far more dramatic than what he'd witnessed a couple of minutes ago. Granted, she was careful, but the more he watched, the more he believed Mercer was right about her feigning the severity of her present condition.

He wished he could figure exactly how much of her memory had returned or how much of the loss had been an act. The same thing with her eyesight. Had it returned?

When he went back inside, Quinn was in the kitchen.

"Hi," she said, setting an unopened envelope on the counter.

Kade walked over, picked it up, and looked at the return address. *LabTech Testing*.

"You ready for this?" he asked.

Quinn shook her head.

"We don't have to open it. Not ever. Whatever is inside that envelope makes no difference to me."

When he set it down, she reached over and picked it up. Rather than opening it, she folded it and stuck it in the back pocket of her jeans. Kade walked over to where she stood and put his arms around her.

"I'm not very good at this," he murmured, breathing in the scent of his daughter, remembering holding her on his lap when she was a little girl.

"What's that?"

"Being a dad."

"I disagree," she said, resting her cheek against his chest. "I think you're very good at it."

Kade closed his eyes and held her tight, regretting every single minute of the last fourteen years he hadn't been a dad to her at all. How much more of his life would he let slip away without living it?

"Throw it away," he said.

"I can't."

Kade let her go and watched as she walked outside and sat with her mother. Whatever the two had to say to each other was none of his business, so he went into the main room, lit a fire, and sat on one of the leather couches that he'd purchased years ago simply because of their size.

He checked his phone, hoping there would be a message from Merrigan. Instead, there was one from Striker.

"Doc, thanks for getting back to me so quickly," he said when Kade returned the call.

"What can I do for you?"

"Sergei Orlov has Fatale."

"What do you mean by he has her?"

"You know damn well what I mean," Striker barked.

Fucking hell. He clenched his fist and looked for something he could throw against the wall. "Where are they?"

"Heading in the direction of Ardrossan."

"Where'd you get your intel?"

"Shiv. He's inside."

"Thank God," Kade muttered. Marquess Thornton "Shiver" Whittaker was one of the best operatives in all the UK.

"What do you want me to do?" Kade asked.

He waited, but Striker didn't respond.

"Say it, Griff."

"I wouldn't think you'd need orders from the agency, Doc."

"Of course I don't." He ended the call and gripped the back of his neck.

"What's going on?" Mercer asked, joining him in the main room of the house.

"I'm heading out."

Mercer nodded. "What can I do?"

"I'm taking Paps and Razor with me."

"I'll handle the details. Where?"

"Glasgow. *Oruzhiye* has Fatale."

"Shit."

Kade walked closer to Mercer and leaned in. "While I'm gone, you figure out what the hell Lena is up to."

"Roger that."

Mercer was already on the phone when Kade went upstairs to get his gear. When he came back down, Quinn was waiting for him.

"You're leaving?"

He nodded. "I'm sorry—"

"Don't apologize. I understand."

"I have no idea how long I'll be gone."

She looked away.

"Quinn? Do you want to open the envelope before I go?"

"No. We'll do it together when you return."

"The guys will meet you at the airfield," said Mercer, who stood a few feet from them.

"The other thing I want you to do while I'm gone is figure out who the hell Animus is," he muttered.

Kade saw Lena out of the corner of his eye, and while she tried to hide, she didn't do it fast enough to keep him from catching her quiet gasp and the way the color had drained from her face.

He leaned into Mercer again. "Find out how Animus and Lena are connected."

Whoever the *sonuvabitch* was, was somehow tied to his ex-wife.

Kade waited until they were on the plane before briefing his teammates on the mission they were about to undertake.

"He's taking her to Arran," said Paps.

"What makes you think so?" asked Razor.

"It's where Fatale is from," he answered.

Kade was surprised Paps knew as much as he did, given he hadn't told them where they were going or why until a few moments ago.

Like Lena, something was off with the man who had been by his side through some of the darkest days of his career. Whatever it was, he couldn't wait any longer to confront him.

Since they'd be in the air for at least fourteen hours, Kade got out a bottle of Scotch, poured three glasses, and handed one to Paps and one to Razor.

"Have a seat, gentlemen."

When they did, Kade proposed a toast. "To lifelong friendship," he said, looking Paps square in the eye.

The man raised his glass and threw back the whiskey. "You ready, Doc?" he asked.

"For what?"

"For me to tell you who I think Animus is."

23

Merrigan

Naturally, the wine list at the Hotel du Vin in Glasgow was outstanding. Merrigan had a difficult time choosing, so when the sommelier approached, she was happy to go with his recommendation.

"I have a terrific sparkling wine from one of England's best, Ridgeview, in Sussex. It's delicious and weighty, made with Pinot Noir and Pinot Meunier. Of course, it's a steal in comparison to vintage champagne."

"That sounds wonderful. Thank you," Merrigan said as she perused the menu. "I'll have the porc et lapin pâté as well." She handed the menu to the somm when he offered to take it.

"Madame, the gentleman seated at the bar asked if he could please take care of your lunch today."

Merrigan looked in the direction the man was pointing and inwardly gasped, recognizing the last person she ever wanted to see again, other than a Maskhadov—Sergei *"Oruzhiye"* Orlov.

That he was here meant she'd made a terrible mistake. She'd inadvertently led a man she was certain wanted to kill her far too close to her childhood home and her sole surviving family members. If her instincts were right, she'd just put her brother, his wife, and their two children in as much danger as she was.

"Fatale," he said, joining her at the table uninvited. "You're looking as beautiful as ever."

Sergei's eyes traveled the length of her body and back, then he smiled when his gaze met hers. "I remember fondly the flush pleasure brings to your face, my dear."

"What a coincidence, running into you in Glasgow," she said, taking a drink from the glass of wine the sommelier set in front of her. She might not have if she hadn't seen him open the bottle and pour directly from it.

"Some say coincidence, some say kismet, *ne tak li?*"

"I wouldn't say either is right, *Oruzhiye.*"

"Happenstance, then."

She nodded, willing her hands not to shake as she took another drink of wine. He was still as devilishly handsome as he'd been the last time she saw him, when she betrayed his love and trust. "Again, what brings you to Scotland?"

"You know the answer, Merrigan."

"I don't."

"Let's say I've been sent to…watch over you."

"Not to kill me?"

Sergei shook his head. "Again, you know better."

"Who sent you?"

He smiled and waved at the waiter, who immediately delivered a chilled bottle of Green Mark vodka, two glasses, and a dish of pickled vegetables.

"Not a chance," Merrigan murmured.

"Ah, but you owe me, *nyet*?" He looked at her in the same way an indulgent parent might look at a child.

She watched as Sergei poured a shot for himself and then for her.

"To your health," he said and threw it back.

Merrigan raised the glass and took a deep breath. It had been a long time since she'd taken the shots this tradition required. She threw it back and watched as he poured another.

"Za nashu druzjbu."

Sergei smirked at her toast to friendship. He waited until she'd downed number two before he did.

"To our love," he countered, pouring and then throwing back the third. He leaned forward, rested his elbows on his knees, and looked into her eyes. "Tell me, Fatale. How is the good doctor?"

"Go to hell, Sergei."

He smiled with tight eyes and studied her. "You're in love with him."

"You know better."

He laughed. "I have missed you."

"Why are you here, *Oruzhiye*?"

"I've already answered that question."

"For whom are you watching over me?"

He smiled. "Perhaps it is just for me."

Merrigan poured another shot for Sergei, then one for herself to mask the chill that ran up her spine. It was her turn to make a toast, but coming up with one was a struggle. As she studied the glass, tears clouded her eyes. "To life," she said, refusing to look at him as she threw back the fourth shot.

"*Lyubov' moya,*" Sergei murmured, reaching over to touch her hand.

"I'm not your love, and I can't do this," she said, pulling her hand away. "Tell me what you want, or say goodbye."

Sergei grabbed her arm and yanked her close enough that she could feel his breath on her skin. "No, Fatale, that is not how this is going down. Not even close."

The ferry had just pulled away from the berth when Sergei parked the car in the waiting lot; it would be close to three hours before the next departure. Merrigan knew this delay hadn't been part of Orlov's plan, and she had no idea what he would do now.

"You aren't a captive, Fatale," he said, likely because of the glare of death she leveled at him.

She held up her hands that were cuffed together. "Are you telling me your sexual proclivities have changed?"

He turned and rested his head against the car window. "You'll see."

"I most certainly will not," she spat at him.

"Settle down. I'm in no mood for your outbursts."

"Then, let me go."

"That, I cannot do."

She looked out her window, then his. "No one is here, it's pitch dark, and the firth sits before us. Why not kill me now?"

"I have said more than once that I'm not going to kill you, Fatale."

"What then, torture? I can assure you I hold little or no information that would be of value to you."

"I cannot believe I told you I missed you less than three hours ago."

"My feelings are mutual. Never seeing you again would've been too soon for me."

He sighed and pulled a bottle of vodka from the backseat. He twisted it open and passed it to her.

"No, thanks. I'd prefer a direct shot to the head over poison."

He took a swig, wiped his mouth with the back of his hand, and handed it back to her. "Drink. You'll need it."

"Where are you taking me?"

Sergei looked in the direction of the ferry's berth and laughed.

"Why the Isle of Arran?"

He shook his head and gave her the indulged-child look for the second time. "I have always found you fascinating, Fatale, but tonight you bore me."

For a few short moments, she'd allowed herself to hope Orlov hadn't discovered that her brother and his family lived on the isle. Now, she knew he had.

"As I said before, let me go."

Sergei sighed, shook his head, and took another swig of the vodka. "You are giving me a headache."

"Just tell me, Orlov. Put us both out of our misery."

"Nyet."

Merrigan folded her arms and looked out the window into the blackness of the night. The conversation they were having was indicative of how their relationship had been since they met when she was a wet-behind-the-ears agent trying to make her mark in MI6. She wouldn't say Sergei was her mentor, necessarily, particularly given he was former KGB and now sold his services to the highest bidder, but they had been lovers for a brief time.

Whether he worked for an ally or an enemy was uncertain and would change depending on who was offering him the most money. He'd said he wasn't going to kill her, which given she was in handcuffs, meant torture was likely on her horizon; it didn't matter how many times he said he was sent to watch over her.

"Tell me what you want to know. I'll save both of us time and me—pain."

Sergei let loose a slew of curse words in his native language, followed by an announcement she hadn't necessarily expected. "As soon as the good doctor arrives, perhaps you will understand."

Merrigan processed his words. Whoever he was working for was either after Doc Butler or wanted something from him. That Orlov had asked about him at the Bistro made more sense. But what did he want from Kade that she wouldn't have or, at least, know about?

"He's made a deal with UR," she said, waiting to see if he reacted, but he didn't.

Instead, he watched, waiting for her to figure it out.

"The Ukrainians," she murmured when it finally dawned on her whom he was working for.

Orlov smiled and nodded.

She should've figured it out sooner. No one hated United Russia more than they did. If the power struggles in Russia were a three-headed monster, UR, Ukraine, and the Maskhadovs would each represent a brain.

"MI6 and the CIA took out the Maskhadovs; now, you want our help taking out United Russia?" The idea was ludicrous. "Not only lofty, impossible."

Sergei didn't respond, but he watched her process through it.

"No, that wouldn't be it, would it?"

The conflict in eastern Ukraine was becoming increasingly violent, with artillery attacks and small arms battles reported daily. Estimated counts were that over ten thousand Ukrainians had been killed by Russian troops in the five-year war being waged in Donbas.

The trade imbalance, however, was Kiev's bigger problem. While Ukrainian exports to the EU were on an upswing, there would never be a fair-trade agreement between them and Moscow. Hardliners pushed for the government to halt all imports from Russia, but the reality was, without those imports, the Ukrainian people couldn't survive. Conversely, the economic sanctions Russia held over them, coupled with their lessening trade exports, were crippling.

If whatever Calder had on United Russia was as big as MI6 and the CIA thought it was, Ukraine could certainly make more use of it than the UK and the US combined.

The possibilities gained from having the upper hand ranged from balancing their trade agreements to ending the war entirely.

"Why would you lure either of us here? What you want is back in the States. By taking us out of the game, you've handed UR easier access."

Sergei's expression turned from amusement, as she continued processing through why he'd abducted her, to a gray and grave-looking mask.

"Animus, you foolish girl."

Merrigan bristled. How was it this man still had enough influence over her that his insults stung?

She should be able to figure out the connection between Kade, her, and the enigmatic Animus. That's what Orlov was trying to tell her.

The abrupt movement of the car jarred Merrigan awake. She rolled her shoulders and attempted to stretch, although the handcuffs didn't allow for much arm movement.

Sergei pulled as far forward as he could on the ferry and turned the engine off. "Welcome back, Sleeping Beauty."

She didn't respond. Her head was pounding, her mouth was dry, and her body hurt all over. She didn't feel like talking.

"Less than an hour, and we'll be in bed."

She turned and glared at him. "*Separate* beds."

He laughed. "What fun will that be?"

"I'll-kill-you-first fun."

"You fell asleep before you figured it out."

Merrigan shrugged. "I have no idea what you're talking about."

"Shall I give you hints?"

She shook her head. "I don't care who Animus is."

"Hmm. I see. Perhaps the good doctor will care more than you do, and he'll play my game."

"Don't let your hopes spiral out of control. I'd lay odds he won't show at all."

"It would be unfair of me to accept your wager. Your wiles have not diminished even though your self-confidence has."

Merrigan shook her head and yawned. "You're boring me, Orlov," she repeated his words to her.

The accommodations the Ukrainians ponied up for shocked her. "This is where you're holding me prisoner?" she asked when he pulled through the gates of Brodick Castle. However, as soon as she said it, she wished she hadn't. It was a bloody medieval castle, for

Christ's sake. The fortress had been around since the fifth century and had a torture chamber and gallows.

"Fatale, as much as I *adore* the sound of your voice, I request that you remain silent."

She raised her arms. "What about these?"

Sergei sighed and glared at her. "I will remove the cuffs; however, if you make a single sound, eye contact, hand gesture, or try to communicate in any way with anyone we come in contact with, I will keep you cuffed to the bed for the duration. Understood?"

She nodded and opened her mouth to speak, but closed it again when he raised his hand.

She remained quiet as they wound their way down the long drive. Even when he drove past the castle itself, she didn't speak. When he pulled up to what had obviously been a caretaker's cottage, she longed to ask about it, but didn't.

After he'd cut the engine, a man approached from the darkness.

"While you are not a prisoner, per se, you are also not free to come and go as you please. Fatale, meet Aleksei. He will ensure you stay put."

Merrigan nodded, but didn't make eye contact with the man Orlov introduced her to. She didn't need to; she'd known him for years.

The two escorted her into the fire-lit cottage. The exterior reminded her of the two on Butler Ranch, which were also built of stone.

Inside, the same stone blended with dark wood beams on the ceiling and walls. The furniture was made from wood and leather, and antler trophies were scattered on the walls. She wondered if this had been the gamekeeper's cottage specifically.

Sergei cleared his throat and motioned for her to come closer. She didn't care for his smirk or the glint in his eye. "Sadly, I am too tired to take you to my bed tonight, *dorogaya.* Perhaps tomorrow."

She was too tired to continue their caustic rapport or even attempt to listen to his conversation with her *guard.* Instead, she asked for the loo.

"Up there," said Orlov, pointing to a closed door at the top of a staircase.

"Thanks," she muttered, taking the slow climb to what she assumed would be her "cell." When she opened the door, she chided herself for mentally complaining. The room was as warm and inviting as the main one downstairs. Another fireplace was lit, and the big bed was covered with Scottish woolen blankets. She appreciated the privacy of the en-suite bath in which sat a claw-foot tub. As welcoming as it appeared, all she really wanted to do was sleep.

She peered out the window after using the lavatory and saw that *Aleksei* was not her sole guard. She closed the curtain and climbed on the bed, crawling under the woolens without removing a stitch of her clothing.

Merrigan opened her eyes, not recognizing the space she was in. It wasn't the room she'd fallen to sleep in, unless she'd been dreaming. The last thing she remembered was arriving at a cottage on the grounds of Brodick Castle and going upstairs to use the loo. She remembered it had a big bed, a lit fireplace, and a claw-foot tub in the adjoining bathroom.

The room she was in now was dark and dank. It had a single bed, one blanket, no fireplace, and certainly no en-suite bathroom. It didn't even have any windows.

She felt groggy, her head hurt, and she was sick to her stomach. Every symptom she had was a side effect of being chloroformed.

When she heard a knock at the door, Merrigan laughed. As if she had any control over who came and went. She heard a key slide into the lock and the door creak open.

"I know you're awake, Fatale," Orlov said, pulling up a chair she hadn't noticed and sitting at the side of the bed. "I'm sorry for the abrupt change of venue, but the good doctor arrived far sooner than expected."

Merrigan put her arm over her eyes. "I thought I wasn't a prisoner, and what the fuck, *Oruzhiye*. Did you have to use chloroform? I would've gone along willingly."

"My apologies. I asked Aleksei to arrange for you to be moved. Whoever he gave the job to was too hasty in completing the task."

Her eyes filled with tears—another side effect of the chloroform. She never would've cried over the situation she was in, particularly when it involved showing that vulnerability to someone like Orlov.

Noticing, he stroked the side of her face with his finger. If she didn't feel like her head was about to explode, she would've jerked away from him.

"*Prosti pozhaluysta,*" he murmured.

"I don't want your apologies, Sergei. Tell me what the hell you're up to instead."

He sighed. "Animus, my dear. Follow along."

"What does Doc have to do with him?"

Orlov raised his eyebrows. "Think, Fatale."

Another knock sounded on the door, and Orlov stood. "Excuse me, *lyubov' moya,* the good doctor has arrived."

24

Kade

He listened to Paps' theory about who Animus was with a mixture of disbelief and concern that his teammate had lost his mind. He couldn't read Razor's expression well enough to know whether he was considering Paps' ideas plausible or also believed the man had gone bonkers.

"Let's consider it one possibility, but continue adding to the list of suspects," Razor said when Paps finished talking.

List? There was one person on it, who was as likely to be Animus as Santa Claus.

"Let's talk about Fatale. Paps, you believe Orlov is taking her to Arran."

"It's the only place that makes sense, Doc."

"If she's still alive," added Razor.

Kade shot him a look.

"Sorry, Doc, but—"

"She's alive," said Paps, looking at his phone. "They're in Ardrossan."

"Where in Ardrossan?"

"You aren't going to believe this." Paps laughed. "They missed the ferry."

"Where are they?" Kade asked for the second time.

"Waiting for the next one."

If Kade had any hair to speak of, he'd be pulling it out at this point. *"Where?"* he bellowed.

Paps held the phone so Kade could see the image Shiver had sent him.

"Jesus Christ," Kade muttered at Orlov's blunder. Sometimes, the wiliest spies made the stupidest mistakes.

"Tell Shiv to shoot the *sonuvabitch* in the head and get Fatale out of there."

Paps shook his head. "No can do."

"Why the hell not? If it's an MI6 thing, call Rivet and tell him to order it."

"It isn't MI6, Doc. It's an Animus thing."

"What do you mean?"

"*Oruzhiye* knows who Animus is."

Doc didn't ask how Paps knew. It was what made all of them good at their jobs. Act on instinct. Don't hesitate, execute. If his teammate's gut was telling him

Sergei knew who Animus was, then Doc also believed he did.

Having a private plane made some things far easier, but not wearing the official badge of the CIA made things like getting through customs a lot more difficult.

"Thanks, Rivet," Kade said, shaking the hand of the man who got them out of red-tape hell.

"Shiv is in place," he responded, holding up his phone, indicating he'd received a message.

"Roger that."

"Let's put this one to bed quickly, gentlemen," Rivet said before departing the plane that would soon be cleared for takeoff to Glasgow.

"By the way," he said, sticking his head back inside, "*Oruzhiye* knows you're on your way."

"Who's on their way?" Paps asked.

"Just Doc. He's the only one Orlov cares about."

Razor laughed. "Thanks."

Kade shook his head. Razor should be thankful *Oruzhiye* didn't give a shit about him or Paps. The man was lethal, primarily because there was no way for them to know whom the man known as "the Gun" was currently working for or what their agenda might be.

Shiv had left Kade a trail a six-year-old could follow. When he drove up to the gate of Brodick Castle, it opened automatically, and he proceeded past the castle itself, to a cottage where he'd been told Orlov was waiting.

"Welcome," Sergei said when Kade climbed out of the car. "You will not be needing your weapons today," he added, expecting him to surrender his gun to one of the four goons surrounding him.

"Where is Fatale?" he asked, keeping his hand on his weapon and leaving no room for Orlov to misunderstand he was refusing to hand it over.

"In due time," he answered, motioning for Kade to follow him into the cottage. "But know this, if you kill me, you and she will also be dead within seconds."

The smirk on the man's face was enough for Kade to consider blowing his head off. "What do you want?" he asked when they sat near the lit fireplace.

Orlov motioned to one of his goons, who brought over a bottle of vodka and two glasses.

"No, thanks," said Kade.

"Do not insult me," he answered, handing Kade the shot glass he'd just poured. "To Fatale's health," he added, raising his own glass.

Kade threw the vodka back at the same time his host did, but did not pour the requisite second round. Instead, he glared at the man and waited.

"Animus," Sergei said, reaching for the bottle.

"What about him?"

Sergei smirked. "I think you know, and your cat-and-mouse game disappoints me greatly. You're getting lazy, just like Fatale. Perhaps it's the lust."

Again, Kade waited, not taking Orlov's bait.

"There is reason to believe the elusive *agent* is someone in your circle. I need what Animus has; you want what I have. Simple."

"Your intel is flawed," said Kade, picking up the bottle and pouring two more shots.

"*Nyet.*" He shook his head. "Of this, I am certain." Orlov again motioned to one of his minions, who soon brought out a charcuterie board.

"Why don't you go after him yourself?"

"Because I do not share the same easy access you do."

"Get to the point, *Oruzhiye*. Who is it, and what do you want me to do?"

"Before I leave, I want to see Merrigan," Kade said later when Orlov escorted him to the door.

"Fatale is perfectly comfortable and happy to have this time to *reconnect*. I'm sure you understand what I'm saying."

Kade was above letting Orlov's insinuation affect him. The ploy was sophomoric at best. While they may have had some kind of dalliance in the past, he didn't doubt Merrigan's disinterest in Orlov was any less than his apathy to Lena.

What did affect him, however, was whom Sergei believed Animus to be. His theory was the same as Paps', and to Kade, it remained ludicrous.

But why would Orlov waste his time by sending him on a wild goose chase? It didn't make sense.

25

Merrigan

"Back so soon?" Merrigan asked, wondering if he'd truly met with Kade when Orlov returned and stood by her bedside.

"Let's go," he said, motioning for her to get up.

"Where now?"

Orlov sighed and grabbed her arm. "You'll see."

He led her through a tunnel as dark and dank as the room she'd been kept in. Her guess was that it connected the castle with its outbuildings. There were several doors, which were probably offshoots leading to other buildings on the grounds. Given she knew the approximate distance between the castle and the cottage they'd initially taken her to, it was easy to deduce that's where he was headed.

By the set of his mouth, she could tell Sergei was angry. Many wouldn't have picked up on the tell, but she'd spent hours—unguarded hours—studying him. She knew him as well as he knew her.

What she hadn't expected was to end up in a garage when they climbed the stairs she'd assumed led to the cottage.

"How was your meeting?" she asked, eliciting the slightest of smiles.

"You well know your importance to the doctor." He stopped walking and turned her to face him. "I once felt the same way he does."

The smile left his face as quickly as it had come. She'd hurt him all those years ago, but worse, she'd betrayed him. When she'd asked if he was there to kill her when he first appeared at the bistro in Glasgow, it was because she'd been expecting him to for years.

"You know that too, don't you, Fatale? That I have feelings for you is the only reason you're still alive."

"You never cared about me."

His grasp on her arm tightened as he pulled her close enough that she could feel his breath. "I loved you," he seethed. "I would've given anything for you, but instead of asking, you *took*."

"You were going to kill me," she whispered. "I heard you."

He let go of her arm and took a step back. "Two things you should've learned from your mistake. First, you know better than to believe everything you hear. Second, even now, your instincts continue to scream of your mistake. You should've trusted them."

"I did, Sergei. That's why I left."

"You didn't *leave*. You absconded with photographs that were worth a great deal of money." He pushed her toward the back passenger door of an SUV.

"I had no choice. The Maskhodovs—"

"Get in," he demanded, not letting her finish her sentence. Once she had, he followed and sat next to her while Aleksei drove and another man sat in the front passenger seat.

"Do you really believe I would've let you live if I did not love you?"

Merrigan looked away when he rested his hand on hers.

"I love you as much now as I did then," he said, quietly enough that she wasn't certain she'd heard him right.

"I apologize, but this is necessary," Orlov said before placing the blindfold over Merrigan's eyes. She should've expected it when he also handcuffed her. "Remember to thank me," he added.

She'd ask what for, but knew she'd find out soon enough.

"How've you been?" asked Merrigan's brother when Orlov left them alone in what she assumed was a safe house.

"I wouldn't begin to know how to answer that. How are you, Mac?"

When he stepped forward and pulled her into a hug, she was almost too stunned to return the affection. She couldn't remember the big, bad MacGregor Shaw ever hugging her before, even at either of their parents' funerals.

"Who's the Russian?" he asked, stepping back.

"If you don't already know, I'll spare you."

"If I didn't want to know, I wouldn't have asked."

This, she was familiar with. Even as adults, they hadn't been able to hold a conversation without exchanging barbs.

"His name is Sergei Orlov. Code name *Oruzhiye,* which directly translates to 'the Gun.'"

"I see."

"Like I said, you didn't want to know. By the way, how did he get you here?"

"He asked if I wanted to see my sister."

"And you just came along?"

He nodded.

"It didn't occur to you that you'd be walking into a dangerous situation?"

"No, it didn't."

"It should've."

"Our lives and our ways of looking at the world are very different."

"You understand now, though."

Mac walked over to the room's window. He drew the curtain back, looked outside, then shook his head and sat back down. "What's this about?"

"I'm a bargaining chip, and unfortunately you are now too."

"Not just me. Mary Pat and the kids are here too."

Merrigan felt as though she was going to be sick. Orlov had found her weakest spot and would use her brother and his family to ensure she did everything he told her to.

"Do you want to see them? I guess I should say meet them?"

"Of course I do, Mac."

"By the way, who's Doc?" he asked.

"What?"

"I asked who Doc is?"

"Why?"

"Oh, for Christ's sake. Because the Russian told me to ask."

"He's an agent. Retired, actually. Former CIA."

"That's it?"

For the second time today, Merrigan's eyes filled with tears, and this time, she couldn't blame the chloroform. How could she explain who Doc was to Mac when she didn't understand their relationship herself?

"He's someone I care about."

"I'd like to meet him someday."

She couldn't help but smile. "I'd like that too. Before you go get them, tell me about your kids."

The conversation she and her brother had was reminiscent of those she'd overheard when Kade took her to meet his family.

"Bronagh turned three last month. She follows her big brother and sister around everywhere. Like you did with me," said Mac.

Merrigan smiled. "Do they hate it as much as you did?"

"More, I think. Rowen tolerates her more than Kevin does."

"You named your son for Da."

"It's his middle name. His first is MacGregor."

"Ah, right. I remember now." Merrigan nodded once.

"Rowan's middle name is Rielle, for Ma."

"How nice. And is Bronagh named for Mary Pat's mother?"

Mac shook his head. "Her middle name is Merrigan."

"Excuse me a moment," she said as she tried hard not to bolt in the direction of the loo before tears threatened.

Mac grabbed her arm and wouldn't let go. "Don't flee, Mer."

She was too choked up to speak and couldn't look at him. "I'm sorry," she finally said. "I don't know why I'm so emotional."

He pulled her back down in the chair. "It's good to see you, Merrigan."

"You too," she murmured, wishing they'd been reunited under different circumstances.

Orlov arrived just as Merrigan, her brother, and his family were finishing dinner.

"Settle your anxiety," he murmured when she took her dishes to the kitchen. "Your family will think you don't want to be with them."

"If you lay a hand on any of their heads, I will ensure you die a slow and very painful death," she seethed as quietly as she could.

She wanted to slap him when he smiled in response.

She returned to the dining room and watched her nieces and nephew, marveling at how the two oldest reminded her of her and her brother when they were young. The other thing that struck her was how openly affectionate her brother was with his wife.

Their family had never been demonstrative, and seeing him so was stunningly brilliant. Part of her hoped she'd have the same kind of relationship, while the other part knew it would be next to impossible. Her living to see another day was unlikely. If, by some miracle, she did, whether she was with Kade or not, she doubted she'd ever be able to lower the walls she'd built with the type of work she did.

"Are you going to kill them?" she asked Sergei on their drive back to Brodick Castle.

"Why do you so quickly question my motives, Fatale, when you should be thanking me?" When he attempted to take her hand in his, Merrigan jerked it away.

"So unappreciative," he muttered, his eyes growing dark. "You'll improve your attitude if you want to see the good doctor ever again."

"Who are you threatening, *Oruzhiye,* him or me?"

"So many tiresome questions for which you already have answers."

"Me, then."

The haunted smile she'd seen frequently since they reunited in Glasgow returned. "*Nyet,* Fatale. *Ya lyublyu tebya.*"

"You don't love me. You wanted to fuck me."

He glared at her.

"Kill me and let my family go."

He shook his head and remained quiet the rest of the ride back.

"Good night, Sergei," she said in a syrupy sweet voice when they arrived at the top of the stairs of the cottage.

"*Nyet* again, Fatale," he said, pushing his way through the bedroom door. "We have things to discuss."

"I'm not letting you fuck me again, Sergei," she said once the door closed behind them.

Orlov got a distasteful look on his face. "Don't be crass."

"Call it whatever you want, but it isn't happening."

"As I remember it, I made you very…happy."

Merrigan folded her arms and stood with her back against the wall.

"Sit, Fatale. We're going to talk, not fuck."

"Who's being crass now?"

Sergei walked to the door and said something she couldn't hear to one of the guards, then came back and sat down. Less than two minutes later, Merrigan heard a knock at the door.

"I'll get it," he said.

As if she were going to offer?

He carried a tray laden with another bottle of vodka and the requisite accoutrements.

"You drink too much, Sergei."

He waved his hand and poured despite her protests.

"Tell me what you know about this woman the doctor was married to."

Merrigan was surprised Orlov knew about her, but she shouldn't have been. "She's Leech Hess' daughter."

"Thank you for telling me something I could easily find on the internet. What else?"

"Why?"

"I'm asking questions. You're answering."

"She dyes her hair and wears too much makeup."

Sergei made what sounded like a growl. "You're testing my patience." He waved his arm again, this time around the room. "Do you prefer your previous accommodations to these?"

She shook her head. "Tell me what you want to know about her."

Merrigan and Orlov talked until after midnight. What had initially felt like a chess match between them had morphed into the familiar witty banter she'd enjoyed with him years ago. There were times it was difficult to remember he was a lethal assassin. However, so was she.

While they didn't stay on the topic long, Merrigan got the impression Sergei's line of questioning about Kade's ex-wife was somehow tied to Animus. He shot down every one of the questions she'd asked that would tell her enough to know for sure, which only convinced her she was on the right track.

"What do you plan to do with my family?"

"Perhaps I'm evening the scale."

Merrigan raised a brow.

"Not in the way you're thinking," he added. "And if tomorrow you repeat the words I'm about to say, I may not continue to be so magnanimous."

She nodded.

"I know why you betrayed me, Fatale. If it were me, I would've done the same. In fact, in my current state of intoxication, I will admit I admired you for it."

She didn't apologize. She couldn't. She wasn't sorry for what she'd done.

"Someday, you will believe I truly loved you," he said and stood.

"I believe it now," she murmured.

He leaned down and kissed her forehead. "Good night, Fatale," he said and walked out of the bedroom.

When Merrigan woke, her mouth felt as though it was filled with cotton, but this time, it wasn't because of chloroform. Instead, it was due to the amount of vodka she'd consumed the night before.

She filled the claw-foot tub she hadn't taken advantage of the first night she'd stayed in this room and sunk into the warm water. While it didn't have jets, the bath reminded her of the last night she and Kade had been together.

He'd carried her body, limp from the pleasure he'd forced from her, and gently set her in the tub that was big enough for both of them.

She closed her eyes and thought about how it felt when she nestled into him and the way his lips had trailed kisses across her back and up the side of her neck. Imagining the love bites he'd scattered on her skin made her shudder.

He'd used his powerful hands to knead her muscles, then his fingers to pleasure her over and over again.

Merrigan moaned as she remembered the way his hardness had felt when she rose, turned around, and straddled him, resting her sex against him until, once again, he filled her in a way no one ever had.

Being with Kade eclipsed every other lovemaking experience she'd had in her life, and she knew no other man would ever touch her body in that way again. Kade was it for her, no matter what happened. If they didn't end up being together, she would remain celibate for the rest of her life.

Merrigan was still in the tub when she heard the bedroom door open and Orlov walk in.

"Get out and get dressed," he snapped, his eyes roaming over the nakedness her bath water did little to hide. "We're leaving."

When he walked from the room, she climbed out and dressed quickly.

"Come with me," he said, grabbing her arm.

"What's going on?" she asked.

"No questions."

Sergei led her out to the upstairs landing and blindfolded her while one of his men cuffed her hands.

"Be grateful there's no chloroform," he grunted.

Someone, probably the same person who'd cuffed her, threw her over his shoulder and carried her down the staircase, through the house, then into the garage.

"Back to the dungeon," she muttered.

"It's for your safety," Orlov answered.

When he removed the blindfold a few minutes later, she saw they'd returned to the dank room.

If Sergei's tone hadn't made his present mood obvious, the set of his face would've.

"What have you done with my family?" she whispered, not wanting to provoke him, but she had to ask.

"They are safe for now, Fatale," he said before leaving without another word.

26

Kade

After his meeting with Orlov, Kade arrived at the designated meeting place before Paps and Razor did, which gave him time to think through their encounter and also about Paps' theory.

Both believed Leech was Animus, and the more he thought about it, the more sense it made.

Leech had initially gone to Russia to find and kill the man who had raped his daughter and betrayed their country.

If he'd found Calder's files, he would've kept them as his own insurance policy. Given he was captured by the last organization he would've wanted to have them, he never would've given away where they were hidden.

But why hadn't he come clean about it in the time since they'd returned to the States? Once Calder's files were in the hands of United Russia, they could all move on with their lives.

"Orlov's theory matches up with mine, doesn't it?" Paps asked when he and Razor arrived.

"He believes Leech is Animus, yes."

"Did you ask him why?"

Kade shook his head. "I didn't ask you either." In fact, he'd dismissed it out of hand so quickly, he hadn't considered doing so.

"There's been traffic between his IP and United Russia," said Paps.

"Do you think he's trying to negotiate something with them?" Razor asked.

"But what?" asked Kade.

"If he's holding out for something they're not willing to give, Barbie being run off the road could certainly be seen as UR firing a shot across the bow."

"We spent days together while she was in the hospital. He wouldn't have been able to hide it from me if that's what he thought."

Paps shrugged.

"What?" Kade asked.

"What about Orlov taking Fatale?"

"You think Leech arranged that as well?" He thought it over for a minute and disagreed. "Orlov said he *needed* whatever Animus had."

"Right," said Paps. "That would leave the circle open, then."

"My guess is he's working for the SBU." The successor of the Ukrainian Soviet Socialist Republic's Branch of the Soviet KGB was the only organization he could think of that would *need* whatever Calder had on UR.

Razor stood and paced the length of the room.

"Talk, Sharp," demanded Kade.

"What you're saying is that Leech found Calder's files and hid them somewhere else, possibly to use as an insurance policy for himself. He was captured, you came after him, and got captured too. Makes sense he wouldn't tell the Maskhodavs where the files were, knowing they'd kill you both once he did. Honestly, that the Russian bad guys held on to the two of you for as long as they did is the most telling proof that Leech *is* Animus. Otherwise, they would've cut their losses."

"Probably would've taken out Barbie and Skipper too, just for the fun of it," Paps added.

Razor stopped pacing and looked at him. "Fatale and UR rescued you, and you made a deal with them to deliver Calder."

Kade nodded. "With you so far."

"Now, we think Leech is making another deal with them, different than the one you made."

Paps nodded.

"You handed over Calder's body to UR, but we know they're on the ground, looking for his files, just like we are. This is where you lose me," said Razor.

"What do you mean?" Kade asked.

"Leech isn't a greedy man. Nor is he any kind of traitor. I don't buy him making side deals."

"Who else would have skin in the game and also have access to Leech's office?"

Paps shook his head. "Anyone with a paper clip. Why Burns hasn't been asked to secure that location is beyond me."

"Until now, we haven't had any reason to," Kade responded.

"The question you should both be asking yourselves is the one I already asked," said Razor. "Who else has skin in the game?"

Kade stayed awake while Paps and Razor slept on the flight back to the States.

The more he turned what they knew about Animus over in his head, the more he believed there was a possibility it could be Leech. However, some of what had been done was sloppy, and even though his former mentor wasn't a technology whiz, he would certainly know better than to allow his IP address to be traced.

Also, his father had been the one to bring the intel to them. If he had any inkling whatsoever that Leech and Animus were one and the same, he would've said so.

"What are you thinking?" Paps asked, stretching his arms over his head.

"It doesn't make sense."

"I hear you."

"It was the internet traffic that led you to believe Leech is Animus?" Kade asked.

"Primarily, but there's more."

"For example?"

"You don't believe his behavior has been odd?"

Maybe so, but the man had spent two years held prisoner. Kade shrugged rather than answer, resting against the seat. "She rescued us," he murmured.

"What's that?"

"Fatale. Orlov has her, and instead of getting her out, I'm flying home to figure out if a man who has been my mentor—practically a second father to me—is ultimately responsible for her abduction."

Kade closed his eyes, picturing Merrigan in bed next to him, her face flush with pleasure, and her sapphire-blue eyes looking deeply into his. He longed to cover her lips with his own and feel her skin flush against his.

He shook his head. If he was going to get her out of Orlov's grasp, he needed to focus on who Animus was and not on missing the woman who held his heart.

"What about Lena's accident? She could've died."

"We've talked about that," Paps answered. "Could've been UR sending a warning."

"They'll answer to me." Kade had promised them everything they wanted, including delivering Calder. In return, they'd given their word that Lena and Quinn would be untouchable. If they didn't honor their side of the bargain, there were plenty of things the agency had promised that would no longer be delivered.

Kade, Paps, and Razor hadn't been off the plane five minutes before they received a message from Mercer, asking them to contact him prior to going to Casa Carrizo.

"What's up, Eighty-eight?" Kade asked.

"You wanted me to find out what Lena had to do with Animus, and I think I've found something. Meet me at the Harmony house."

"Roger that."

"Think he found a connection to Leech too?" Paps asked.

Kade shrugged. "On one hand, I hope so. On the other…"

"I hear ya."

Before they got halfway to Harmony, Kade received another message, this time from Leech, telling him it was urgent he speak with him.

Where are you? Kade messaged and waited.

"Pull over," he told Paps. If Leech wanted them to meet him in Montecito, he didn't want to get any further north.

"I'll let Eighty-eight know we'll give him a status update in a few," said Razor.

Lifeguard stand 27, Leech replied.

He showed Paps the message.

"Change of plans. Leech has requested a meeting," Paps called Mercer and told him.

"I see," he answered. "Level of urgency?"

"He's asking us to meet him at the beach in Montecito, so somewhere without ears."

"I'm on my way," Mercer confirmed.

"What do you think this is all about?" Paps asked Kade after he hung up.

"Eighty-eight must've found proof, and Leech must know it."

As much as Kade would've preferred to wait until Mercer arrived before talking with Leech, he could see the man waiting near the lifeguard stand.

"I'll go. You two and Eighty-eight join me when he arrives."

Paps and Razor both nodded.

The farther he went in the sand, the heavier his legs felt to him. It was as though he was carrying a boulder that grew bigger with every step. That Leech wanted to meet somewhere like this was as telling as it was worrisome.

When he approached, Leech turned away from him and looked out at the ocean.

"Talk to me," said Kade.

"I've always tried to do my best for my country and my family. You know that, right?"

"Yes. I do."

"There have been times when I've been blindsided by things I never could've predicted happening."

"All of us have."

"Not to the same degree."

Kade wished Leech would get to the point, but he could hear the agony in the man's voice, and waited for him to be ready to confess whatever he was here to say.

"There hasn't been a day in the last twenty-two years when I haven't wished I could go back and undo the events of that night."

Kade nodded, knowing he was referring when Calder had raped his daughter.

"The decisions I made set so many things in motion. Devastating things."

"You had no control over what happened. It would've been worse if you'd allowed Calder to continue in the program."

"I agree. More of our agents would've been in jeopardy, even killed, if I had."

"What have you done, John?" Kade asked. This was not a time for code names. This was a conversation between two men who meant a lot to each other, regardless of the work they did.

"It isn't me."

"Who, then?"

Leech's voice caught, and Kade waited for him to continue.

"My daughter."

Kade felt a chill spread throughout his body. "What has Lena done?"

Leech put his head in his hands. "I don't have proof…"

"I do," said Mercer, who had walked up with Paps and Razor.

Leech startled. "When the hell did you get here?"

"Just now, sir," answered Paps.

"What have you got, Eighty-eight?" Kade asked.

"I brought the laptop."

Kade looked at Leech. "Can we go back to the house?"

"There's something else I need to tell you first," he answered.

"What?"

"Barbie's gone, isn't she?" Paps asked.

Leech nodded.

Kade gripped the back of his neck. "When?"

"I went to check on her this morning, and she wasn't in her room. I thought maybe she had a doctor's appointment, but when Quinn came downstairs, she said she didn't," Mercer told them.

"The nurse is gone too?"

"Affirmative," he answered.

When they returned to his house, Kade went upstairs to look for Quinn.

She was standing in the doorway of her bedroom when he reached the top. When he opened his arms, she walked into his hug.

"How are you?" he asked.

She shook her head, and he could feel the dampness of her tears on his shirt. "My mom…she faked all of it."

"You saw her that night, Quinn. While we don't know exactly when her condition began to improve in earnest, we both know she didn't fake the accident."

"Mercer told me he was watching her."

"How do you feel about that?"

Quinn shrugged. "I'd been watching her too. When we brought her here…Well, I wasn't convinced she was as bad off as we thought."

"We have reason to believe your mother has gotten mixed up with some very dangerous people. What we're trying to ascertain right now is how deep and what kind of trouble she's in."

She nodded and turned away from him. "I'm so sorry."

Kade gripped her shoulders. "Look at me. You have no more reason to apologize for your mother's actions than I do, or than Leech does."

"It's just that…"

Kade shook his head. "It's just that…nothing. You know who could really use your support right now?"

"Who?"

"Your grandfather."

Quinn's tear-filled eyes met his.

"Mercer, Paps, Razor, your grandfather, and I have a lot to discuss—things it would probably be better if you didn't know."

"I'm good at not asking questions."

"Yeah?"

"Mercer's been telling me to trust him since the day I met him. He has this way, you know? When *something's* going on, I can just tell."

He smiled. "Can you read me too?"

"Not as well as Paps and Razor."

Kade kissed her forehead. "We'll talk more later."

She nodded, went into the bedroom, and closed the door.

"When's the last time anyone saw Barbie?" Paps was asking Leech when Kade joined them.

"Last night around ten."

"Was that the usual routine?"

"More or less. At least one of us checked in on her before we called it a night," answered Leech.

Mercer nodded. "I left at zero five hundred this morning and didn't think to look in on her."

"I'm sure she was already gone," said Kade.

Leech nodded and put his head in his hands like he'd done at the beach. "The accident?"

"My guess is United Russia," said Mercer. He turned to Kade. "Not because they reneged on your deal. I think she might've been playing two sides against the middle."

Mercer opened his laptop. "Shortly after you left for Scotland, I started running surveillance on several places, including the Harmony house. It became obvious to me within days after Lena was released from the hospital, that her recovery was going much more quickly than she'd admit. I believe she had at least partial vision right away. And I'm not sure she ever suffered memory loss. I found this earlier." He played a video showing Lena and another woman enter the house in Harmony and go into the kitchen.

"Who's that?" asked Paps. "The new nurse?"

"Yep."

They watched as Lena used a key to open the door to the room Mercer used as his bedroom and office. From there, the two did a thorough search, opening drawers and rifling through what was in them. They even checked the floor and closet.

"What are they looking for?"

"What we found in the cabin," Paps answered.

The four men turned and looked at him. Paps wouldn't look any of them in the eye.

"Before the accident, we uh…spent some time together. I helped her find the house in Summerland. Stuff like that," he told them.

"It was more than that, wasn't it?" Kade asked.

Paps shook his head. "It probably would've been, but she started asking questions about what else was in the cabin."

"Stop right there," said Leech, holding up his hand. "What she was looking for wasn't in the cabin; it was here."

"What do you mean?"

"I hid it here, and she found it."

"When?" Mercer asked.

Leech shrugged. "When she wasn't here this morning and Quinn didn't know where she was, I went and looked, and it was gone."

"How in the hell did she get in contact with United Russia?" Kade asked.

"I did a thorough search of Leech's computer," said Mercer, who then looked at the man. "Sorry, sir."

"Apology accepted. I figure you're one of the good guys."

Mercer continued. "From what I can tell, she's been at this since we returned from Europe with Leech. UR issued an ultimatum right before the accident, demanding delivery."

Kade stood, wanting to hurl something through the wall. What in God's name had she been thinking?

"I'm not sure they intended to run her off the road. They may have planned to scare her, but things went too far."

Kade felt sick to his stomach. "What is she getting in exchange?"

Mercer scrubbed his face. "What I'm about to say is something I've spent hours thinking through."

Kade nodded.

"Fatale."

His stomach lurched. *"Fucking find Lena,"* he bellowed.

"On it, Doc," said Paps, who was already messaging his contacts at various checkpoints.

At the same time, he knew Mercer and Razor were reaching out to their people at TSA.

Kade rested his hand on Leech's shoulder. "This is not on you. I'm just as responsible, or more."

"Bullshit," spat Leech, shirking away from Kade's grasp. "I rue the day I ever set eyes on Rory Calder."

"None of us feel differently."

"But this isn't just on Rory's head. Her mother and I have pushed you and Lena to be together since the day you showed up at our place on Old Creek Road."

"There was a time we both went along with it willingly," said Kade. "But things changed. Connect the dots for me, though, Leech."

"I'm hypothesizing, but it isn't difficult to figure out my daughter wanted to get rid of whatever stood between you and her being together. That's Fatale. Lena's been around the game long enough to know how it's played. Offer a good enough deal, and you can make whatever you want happen."

"Tell me what she's got," said Kade.

"Names, kill dates, and who was responsible."

Jesus. Kade didn't even want to ask, but he had to. "Is Vinogradoff responsible for at least one of the hits?"

"Far more than that. At least half."

Tikhon Vinogradoff was the current Russian president and had been a KGB foreign intelligence officer for sixteen years, rising to the rank of lieutenant colonel before resigning to enter politics. If *proof* got out that he was personally responsible for killing any CIA operatives, let alone the number he had, United Russia's relationship with the United States would cease to exist.

"Do you have another copy anywhere?"

Leech nodded and pulled something out of his pocket. "If I'd died, you would've been contacted."

Kade knew what he was looking at because he'd received the same kind of thing many times over the course of his career.

The original document Leech had turned in was registered with the Central Intelligence Agency of the United States. What Leech had handed to him was a card bearing the seal of the agency, with a set of numbers printed on it. Once contacted, Kade would've had to supply the agency with those numbers as verification in order to be given access to the documents Leech had surrendered. However, without the proper security clearance, he would've been denied regardless.

"Did you hide the other stuff Quinn and Eighty-eight found in the cabin?" Razor asked.

"Affirmative," Leech responded.

Kade wanted to know how he'd gotten his hands on a lot of it, but at this point, it no longer mattered. Quinn knew the circumstances of her birth. Everything else she and Mercer found had little significance.

"Let's move out," suggested Razor. "We don't have time to waste."

Kade agreed. They should be ready to leave the minute they learned Lena's whereabouts.

"Leech?"

"Do what you need to do," he told Kade.

"I'm sorry."

"You didn't do this. I did."

The team was on the plane, waiting to file their flight plan.

"We're gonna have to sell United Russia something of our own to pay the jet fuel bill," joked Razor. "Here's an idea. You could hand over Orlov."

Kade grunted. Jokes were his friend's way of trying to alleviate the tension. However, he wasn't sure yet whether the Russian was on UR's payroll.

"We know Fatale's being held somewhere in Brodick Castle, but even Shiver doesn't know where," Razor muttered.

"Where the hell is Lena? That's what I want to know first," Kade barked.

"Headed to Glasgow," said Mercer, standing up with his own laptop and pointing to the email confirming her travel with Zaryana Ivashov—according to facial recognition. He'd also received surveillance footage of them at the Los Angeles airport terminal.

"She's traveling under one of the assumed identities we gave her," said Mercer.

"She knows enough to be dangerous to herself and us, but not enough to cover her tracks," added Paps, shaking his head. "If you're right about her travel companion, there is a good chance Barbie isn't going of her own accord."

Kade had heard of Ivashov, code name *Raketa*, which directly translated to "Rocket" in Russian. From what he understood, she was one of KGB's best.

"We're set to roll," said Razor, coming back from the cockpit. There were three pilots on K19's rotation. Today, Montano "Onyx" Yáñez was the plane's captain while Manon "Alegria" Mondreau was his copilot. Both were trusted operatives who had run several missions with the team.

"When this is over, I want to talk about K19," said Paps.

Kade nodded, fastening his seat belt. "We can talk now," he answered, motioning to the seat next to him.

Paps, in turn, motioned to Razor, who sat across from them.

"What about Eighty-eight?" he asked.

"I'm right here," answered Mercer, sitting down in the fourth seat.

"Razor and I have discussed it at great length. We know you both want to retire," Paps began, looking between them. "However, neither of us do."

Kade nodded.

"I know I said it was all or none…"

"But we changed our minds," said Razor with a toothy grin. "We're not done savin' the world."

"I have to admit I've been giving it some thought…" said Kade.

"And?"

"I'm done traveling the world for the job, but I think I can help save a few lives from the comfort of my office."

"I hear ya," said Paps, looking at Mercer, who hadn't said anything yet.

"I'm out," he answered. "I made a promise."

"What about forensics?" Razor suggested.

Mercer raised his head. "Maybe."

Kade smiled when Mercer did. He would guess that his future son-in-law felt much the same way he did. It was one thing to say you're retiring and getting out of the game entirely, but actually doing it was much harder.

"We've been askin' around. Some of the crew have expressed an interest in coming on board in a greater capacity," Razor told them.

"Who?" asked Kade.

"Today's pilot and copilot have both added their names. Plus…"

Kade caught the look that passed between Razor and Paps. *"Who?"*

"Striker."

"No."

"You get one vote, Doc. That's the way it works," said Paps.

Kade looked at Mercer.

"I don't have anything against him, to be honest with you."

"Shit. Who else?" Kade grumbled.

"Dutch."

He remembered the man who he'd thought had taken it upon himself to have the cloth used to knock out either his father or Quinn analyzed. While his father said he'd given him the orders to do it, Kade didn't like that he hadn't gone through the proper chain of command.

"Anyone else?"

"Mantis."

He was the third pilot on K19's roster. "Is that it?"

"We were thinkin' Fatale might want to sign on, but…"

"Have you always done this?" Kade asked Razor.

"What?"

"Not finished your sentences. It's like you're a seven-year-old."

Razor laughed and looked at Paps. "Told you he'd be a dick about it. We figured if we saved her ass, she might want to come on board."

"First we have to actually save it, and then…Rivet might not be so ready to let her go."

"You two are the real deal, though, right?" Razor's smile left his face, and he looked into Kade's eyes.

"I sure as hell hope so."

Each member of the K19 team retreated to seats away from one another to think through their course of action once they were on the ground. Soon, they'd gather again and solidify each phase of their plan.

"Ready?" Kade asked an hour later.

"Yep," answered Razor, who came back to sit across from him.

"What've you got?"

"Hang on," he answered, motioning for Paps and Mercer to join them.

Razor laid out the map and marked where each of them should go in.

"Where's Shiv?" Kade asked.

"Inside, but Orlov's kept him away from Fatale," he answered.

"Eighty-eight, you stay here," Kade said, pointing to their rendezvous spot.

Mercer shook his head. "Put one of MI6's people there."

While Kade was more than willing to risk his life to save the love of his, he wouldn't allow his daughter's to do the same. He needed to know Mercer would be there to take care of Quinn in the event something happened to him.

"I can't do it, Eighty-eight. Don't ask me to," Kade implored, hoping his teammate understood just how difficult this was for him. "I'm essentially clipping your wings, and I know it. But—"

Mercer nodded. "I don't like it, but I get it."

As they ran through the rest of the plan, Razor made adjustments based on Mercer's change of involvement.

"All set?" Kade asked anxiously.

His three teammates nodded.

"Let's talk about Lena, then." Kade looked at Paps.

"I believe that United Russia 'summoned' her."

Kade nodded. "Formally escorted."

"Raketa Ivashov is one of the best agents we've seen out of the KGB in the last twenty years."

"She doesn't look very old," commented Razor.

"She isn't." Paps focused on the screen of his laptop. "Thirty."

"Let's get her."

Kade understood why Razor suggested it, and maybe years ago, he would've agreed. Now, all he cared about was getting Merrigan safely out of Scotland. Capturing a Russian assassin and convincing her to become a double agent was beyond what he was willing to do.

"Before you comment," added Razor, winking. "You get one vote."

"Back to Barbie," Paps muttered. "UR doesn't trust her."

"They're waiting to get their hands on what she's got before they honor their side of the deal," said Kade.

"Exactly. Once Lena hands off the evidence Calder had on Vinogradoff, Fatale's kill order will immediately go into effect."

"Unless Orlov intercepts her first."

Vinogradoff himself certainly wouldn't show. Instead, his second-in-command would confirm the authenticity of Animus' delivery and issue the order to kill the woman whom Kade knew he couldn't live without.

"On the other hand, they may kill Lena first and let Fatale go."

Kade had thought of that too but couldn't bring himself to say it out loud. What kind of a man did it make him to hope they did and left Merrigan alone?

"Have we heard from MI6?" he asked.

"Affirmative," answered Razor. "We'll be on the ground in Glasgow before the flight Lena and her escort are on is permitted to leave Heathrow."

"And backup?"

"Already on their way to the castle."

Kade closed his eyes, willing Merrigan to keep herself safe until he got to her.

Why in God's name hadn't he been brave enough to tell her how much she meant to him when they were last together? Had she been able to feel his love for her as he showed it with his hands, his mouth, his body? Three simple words would've ensured she'd know the depth of his feelings for her. Why hadn't it been so simple then?

If, by the grace of God, he held her in his arms in the next few hours, they would be the very first words he'd utter.

27

Merrigan

Merrigan could hear Orlov cursing, but not much more of the conversation he was having with Aleksei—who she hadn't seen or heard anything from in days—and her other "guards" on the opposite side of the thick wall separating her room from the hallway. She jumped when the door burst open and Sergei walked in.

"You're staying here for the time being." He sat on the bed, beside her. "I told you before, but you didn't believe me. Now, you must understand that I brought you here for your own good."

"What about my family, Sergei?"

"Rivet is aware of your family's whereabouts."

She nodded and looked into his eyes. "Tell me what's happening."

"Animus is on the way. So is United Russia."

This didn't make sense. UR had helped MI6 infiltrate the Maskhadovs, then helped get Kade and Leech out. The blood of the few remaining members of their mortal enemy was shared between all three teams—UR, MI6, and K19.

"I don't understand. UR and MI6—"

"Things have changed."

"In what way?"

"Animus wants your head, and UR has committed to delivering."

"Mine? Why?"

Orlov shook his head. "You will understand soon enough."

"What about K19?"

"They fucking better be on their way to stop them."

"Can't you stop them?"

"I have other matters to attend to. While K19 keeps United Russia busy and prevents them from killing you, I intend to take Animus."

"Take?"

"Like I've said several times, Animus has what I want. And I have what the good doctor wants. If things go as I hope, we'll both be happy."

"And United Russia?"

"Their losses will be…unfortunate. However, if Animus has what I think she has, UR will be in no position to do anything but give in to every Ukrainian demand, regardless of what happens here today."

"Did you say 'she'?"

Orlov nodded.

Who the hell was this Animus, and why had she put a bounty on Merrigan's head?

She put her fingertips to her temples, wishing she could magically stop her head from throbbing. It was too difficult to think through the pain of it.

"Go with Aleksei," Orlov said two hours later when he unlocked the door of the room where Merrigan was being held captive.

"Sergei?" she whispered.

"What is it?"

"Be careful."

He closed his eyes for just a moment, and when he opened them, she knew. Sergei *had* loved her all those years ago, and loved her still.

"Godspeed, Fatale," he murmured, cupping her cheek briefly before he kissed her forehead and walked out of the room.

The man Orlov referred to as "Aleksei" waited outside the cell until he was certain Sergei was gone, then he came inside and shut the door.

"Bring me up to speed, Shiv," said Merrigan.

The MI6 operative who had successfully infiltrated Orlov's team gave her a rundown of what he knew of Sergei's plan. Everything Shiv told her confirmed what Sergei himself had said. His intention was to intercept Animus while relying on K19 to keep UR at bay long enough for him to get his hands on the documents she was delivering.

"And then he'll kill her," she added.

"She isn't traveling alone. She's being escorted by one of UR's best."

"Who?"

"Raketa Ivashov."

Shite. "And me?"

"Orlov has not given an order where you're concerned."

"My family?"

"As difficult as it is for anyone who knows him to believe, I am convinced Orlov's intention is to keep them safe. K19 should be on the ground now," he added.

Praying Shiv was right, at least for the time being, Merrigan was ready to put her own plan together. If only there weren't so many players and moving parts to keep track of.

She needed to focus on one goal only: to be the first to find Animus and kill her and Ivashov before they killed her. From there, she'd make her own deal with United Russia. In exchange for turning over everything Calder had on them, she, the rest of the MI6 team, and K19 would walk away unscathed.

That left only Orlov. Merrigan knew Shiv's plan was to take him out too, unless UR did it first. It was something she had to accept. In the end, it would be either her or him. If allowed to live, he'd never forgive her for this second betrayal. He'd kill her, then ensure everyone she cared about was taken out as well, not just her family, but Doc Butler too.

"Ready?" Shiver asked, handing her a gun and leading her out of the room and down the stone corridor.

"One last thing. Who the hell is Animus?"

28

Kade

Kade, Razor, and Paps had just entered the tunnels when they heard a shot fired.

"I'll take this one," Kade yelled. *"You two go that way."*

Razor and Paps ran down the right path while Kade ran to the left. He'd memorized the layout of the castle's tunnels and knew both main corridors led to the dungeon where Shiv reported Merrigan was being held.

They'd agreed that rescuing her was their primary mission, leaving the MI6 team to deal with Orlov, Animus, and United Russia.

Rescue. He prayed that's what he was doing. Kade couldn't let himself think about the one shot they'd heard. He couldn't accept that single gunshot meant *anything.* Shiver was with her, wasn't he? Wouldn't that mean that if, God forbid, Animus, Raketa, or anyone else had fired, Shiv would've fired back? He told himself that lack of additional rounds had to be a good thing.

Kade rounded each curve in the tunnel with expedient caution, wishing they'd been able to figure out how to get a comms set to Shiver.

The corridor he was in ended in a T he didn't remember from the map. He closed his eyes, trying to recall which way would take him to the dungeon.

29

Merrigan and Shiv went dead silent when they heard the single shot fired. Given there wasn't anywhere close for them to hide, they stood in place, waiting until they heard something else—*anything* else.

"Let's go," Shiver whispered after a few minutes passed.

Merrigan nodded, wanting to be out of these corridors where anyone could corner them.

When they heard footsteps a few minutes later, they both froze, leveling their guns before Shiver took two tentative steps forward and she went to the right. From that vantage, she'd see whoever it was first and could get the first shot off. Shiv would then immediately fire the second at closer range.

They both heard the quiet, slow tapping of a foot and lowered their guns just as Paps and Razor rounded the corner.

Paps mouthed, "Shot?"

"We heard it too," whispered Merrigan, motioning to a different corridor with her head.

Paps nodded, going first. She followed with Shiv and Razor behind her. Slowly, they made their way, hesitating with each turn, four guns leveled.

"Shit," Paps gasped when they saw the body. He moved forward and carefully rolled the woman over while the other three covered him.

He felt for a pulse and nodded. "Raketa," he whispered, then examined her body for the wound.

Merrigan knew the minute he found where the bullet had hit, then watched as he looked for an exit wound, shaking his head moments later.

Raketa was still alive, which meant the bullet had either grazed her skull or was still lodged in her brain. If it was the latter, the chance she'd survive was slim. Without immediate medical attention, however, it would be null.

Before Paps could move her, Raketa's eyes fluttered open.

"Fuck," they heard her mutter, trying to sit up.

"Stay still," Paps whispered, motioning for them to go ahead.

"Animus." She groaned, pointing in the opposite direction from where Merrigan, Shiv, and Razor were headed.

If it were solely up to her, she wouldn't trust Raketa, but it wasn't, and Razor and Shiver appeared to be contemplating which way to go.

"Let's split up," Razor suggested. He went in the original direction while she and Shiver went where Raketa pointed.

"Go," she heard Raketa say to Paps, but he shook his head, looking conflicted.

"Do what you think is best," Merrigan said before following Shiv.

When that corridor came to a T, they split up. Merrigan went right; Shiv went the other way. At this point, they just needed to find Animus and neutralize her. They knew she had no backup, so it wasn't as though they'd be outnumbered, unless of course, UR had found her and were looking for Merrigan to fulfill their side of the agreement.

Razor had told them Kade was somewhere below ground too, and where Orlov was, was anyone's guess. The entire dungeon level was a potential minefield.

Merrigan could hear footsteps not far from where she was. She scooted tight against the wall, gun leveled, until she could see around the corner, and was about to proceed when she heard a voice say, "Just the person I'm looking for."

When Merrigan spun around, Lena was standing in front of her, holding the same gun she'd probably used to shoot Raketa.

"*You're* Animus?" Merrigan gasped.

"That's right," said the last woman she expected to see pointing a gun at her. "You all underestimated me, even the Russians."

Lena looked very pleased with herself, but there was something else Merrigan saw. Looking into the woman's eyes, she could tell she was operating on pure adrenaline, but worse, she saw madness.

"You don't have to do this," she began. "If it's Kade you want, you've got him. He and I have nothing—"

"*Shut up,*" Lena shouted at her. "Don't talk to me about Kade. I've loved him my whole life, and he loves me. He always has. I don't need you to give him up."

"Then, what is it you want?" Merrigan kept talking, hoping someone would hear them and give her backup.

"I don't ever want to see your face again."

From where she stood, Merrigan could see the hammer of the gun was cocked and the safety was off. If Lena got the shot off, it would be a tossup as to whether she could as well.

Before either could do anything, she heard Kade's voice from behind her.

"Don't do it, Lena. Put the gun down. *Now.*"

"Her gun is pointed *at me*. Why aren't you telling *her* to put the gun down?"

Merrigan lowered it without him needing to ask.

"What are you doing?" Kade said in a soft voice as he rounded slowly past Merrigan toward his ex-wife. His words didn't soothe her, though, and Lena leveled her gun at him.

"Don't come any closer," she warned. *"Not another step."*

Kade froze and held one hand up while the other still held his gun. Merrigan raised hers again as well.

"This isn't going to end well for you unless you give up your gun and take a walk with me, Lena."

When she closed her eyes momentarily, Merrigan knew she was about to fire. Before she could get a shot off, Lena did, and Kade fell to the ground.

"Freeze!"

Merrigan could feel the person step up behind her and knew Paps had a gun too, also leveled at Lena.

"Don't do this, Lena. If you think I won't shoot, you're wrong."

Lena's eyes darted between Merrigan, Paps, and Kade, who was on the ground, holding his leg, his gun still pointed at her.

Lena took another deep breath and closed her eyes. Before she could get the second shot off, Merrigan heard the *ptew* of a gun being fired over her shoulder and watched Lena crumble to the ground.

Paps raced around her and caught the woman in his arms before her head hit the concrete, but there was no question she was dead; he'd hit her square in the chest with a .45. No one could survive a shot like that.

Merrigan ran to where Kade sat, holding his leg. "What can I do?" she asked.

"Didn't hit the femoral artery, so I'll live," he said, looking over at Paps.

"Goddammit," they heard him cry over and over again, still holding Lena in his arms.

"Paps," yelled Kade. "Listen to me. We need to get out of here, and I need your help."

It took a couple of seconds, but Paps' eyes focused on Kade's at almost the same time Razor and Shiver rounded the corner.

"*Shit!*" Razor yelled when he saw Lena first, then Kade holding his leg.

"Raketa?" Paps asked him.

"UR has her," he answered, then looked at Merrigan. "They got Orlov too."

"Is he…"

"Between the eyes."

The familiar pang hit her square in the chest even knowing he'd done it to himself by making the choice to do what he did for a living. Thinking any of them could come out of this unscathed, would've been naive, and that's the last thing she was.

"My family?" she said to Shiver.

"Rivet's got them." He looked at his watch. "Should be safely in London by now."

"Thank God," she murmured, closing her eyes and imagining the sweet faces of her nieces and nephew. If anything had happened to them, she'd never forgive herself.

"You steady?" Razor asked as he helped Kade up. "Can you make it outta here?"

Kade didn't respond. Instead, he motioned to Merrigan. "Come here."

He pushed Razor away when she was close enough to walk into his open arms.

"I promised myself that this would be the first thing I said to you today." He looked into her eyes. "I love you, Merrigan. I don't want another minute to pass without you knowing I do."

"I love you, Kade."

"They're at Vauxhall Cross," Shiver told her when the plane landed.

Merrigan nodded. "I'll just…"

Shiver folded his arms. "I'll just taxi you over." He smiled.

"That would be great. Thank you."

God, what was she going to say to them? *Sorry. I almost got you killed, but it was nice seeing you again.* Maybe they wouldn't even want to see her. They could return to their simple life on the Isle of Arran, back to the precious little stone cottage she assumed they lived in, and do their best to forget their Aunt Merrigan even existed.

"Maybe they won't want to see me," she said when Shiver pulled up in front of MI6's headquarters.

He smiled. "They've been asking for you."

"Who has?"

"All of them, according to Rivet, but the little ones have been relentless."

"Why?"

Shiver smiled. "Because you're a delightful human being."

She laughed. "That's rubbish."

Regularly facing down criminals who wanted to kill her didn't make Merrigan as nervous as she was in anticipation of facing her brother. If she were him, she'd banish herself from their lives forever, and maybe that was what he planned to do.

"Stop it," Shiv said as he held her car door open. "You look scared to death, and I can speak from experience in saying that will not endear you to children."

"Thank you for the ride." She kissed his cheek, then walked inside to the lift, where she pressed the seventeenth floor.

"It'll be brilliant," he said as the door closed behind her.

Wiping her sweaty hands on her pants, Merrigan took a deep breath, then blew it out slowly, willing the lift to slow down.

On the walk to Rivet's office, she felt the same way she would if she were about to be reprimanded.

"Merrigan!" her brother shouted when she opened the door, running over to hug her.

"Merrigan, Merrigan, Merrigan!" the little ones chorused after their father, then ran to put their arms around her legs. When she caught her sister-in-law's eyes, she saw tears, but she was also smiling.

"We're so glad you're safe," said Mary Pat. "That's *Auntie* Merrigan," she playfully scolded her children.

"Where are you staying?" she asked once the raucous had settled.

Mac shrugged. "We didn't get that far."

"I have a flat here in London."

"We wouldn't want to impose," said her brother's wife.

"No imposition whatsoever. I do have a guest room, although you'd be the first to sleep in the bed. The kids can take my room if that works."

"The kids can sleep with us or whatever other accommodations we can patch together. They're *not* taking your bed," said Mac. Her brother put his arm around her. "We were so worried," he murmured.

Merrigan didn't know what to say. The events of the past week weren't much different than what she'd experienced on any other mission. Only that he had an inkling of the danger she faced made it unique.

"Shall we, then? I'll just pop in and thank"—she looked over at the children—"Sir Ranald."

"Sir?" asked Kevin, whose eyes lit up.

"Indeed. He's been knighted by the Queen herself."

"Wow," her nephew mouthed as Merrigan bypassed his secretary and rapped on Rivet's door.

"Enter," he bellowed.

"Thank you for this, sir."

Rivet looked away from his computer screen and at her. "I want you to take some time away."

"Meaning?" Was he reprimanding her?

"Don't get your knickers in a knot. I'm merely suggesting you take some time off."

"Yes, sir," she answered with heated cheeks.

"And, Fatale, try to figure out what you want to do with the rest of your life."

"Are you *firing* me?"

"On the contrary. I'm suggesting there may be other opportunities ahead of you that you may find more…appealing."

Merrigan sat in the chair in front of Rivet's desk. "What's this, then? Why are we having this conversation?"

Rivet came around and leaned against the front of his desk. "Life, Merrigan. Don't forget to live it."

She nodded, looking into his warm eyes. "Thank you, Riv."

"Away with you now. It is my understanding that a certain retired CIA agent is desperately trying to reach you. In fact, I'll step out, and you can ring him now."

"That isn't necessary—"

"Oh, my dear, it certainly is. If you don't contact him soon, I'm afraid he'll descend on my office."

30

Kade

"How are you holding up?" he asked Paps once they were en route to London.

"I cared about her," he answered. "It fucking kills me that I had to be the one."

"I know." Kade rested his hand on Paps' shoulder. "I don't know if I could've done it if I thought about it."

"That's what we're trained for, Doc. Don't think, just kill."

That wasn't all they were trained for, but Paps didn't need a dressing down from him now. All he needed was for Kade to listen. Every single kill was tragic; each one took a little bit more of the shooter's soul, even if it was kill or be killed.

Kade couldn't wait to get to the airfield, find Merrigan and bask in the goodness he knew lived inside of her.

Shiver had whisked her away far too quickly. The goodbye they'd said to one another was fleeting, neither knowing when they'd see each other again, only that it had to be *soon*.

The evidence against United Russia that Calder had held onto all those years was in their hands now, but no one in Russia's FSB would be naive enough to think there was no other copy.

No formal agreement had been made, and UR had left Scotland, knowing that both the CIA and MI6 continued to hold something potentially devastating to Russia's current ruling political party.

At some point, the bureaucrats would make it official, but for now, Kade knew he could rest assured there was no longer imminent danger hovering over his family.

Soon, he'd have to call Leech and tell him Lena was dead. Regardless of what she'd done, she was still his daughter. He would be understandably heartbroken, which left Kade feeling that way too.

"Let me do it," said Paps.

"Call Leech?"

"Yeah."

"You don't have to. I'll—"

"I want to, Doc. More, I need to."

"Understood."

That left Quinn, and Kade had to be the one to tell her. This wasn't something she could hear from anyone else.

The call could wait, though, until he was alone in his hotel room, and then, he'd make it a video call. Not knowing when he'd be back in the States, it was something he couldn't put off.

"Chopper's on its way," Razor said to both him and Paps. "It will take us from Heathrow to the helipad at MI6 headquarters."

Kade's relief was palpable when he saw Merrigan's name flash on his screen just as the helicopter landed. "Hi," he answered.

"I understand you've been pestering my boss," she teased.

"I won't apologize."

"Very well. I suppose, then, I should invite you… Oh, wait…I've just invited my brother and his family to stay at my flat."

"Are you heading there now?"

"Yes, but—"

"On my way."

Kade had made arrangements for the team to stay at Dorchester's Forty-Five Park Lane, and while he booked a room for himself, he hadn't planned to use it. Perhaps he would, after all.

Having Merrigan in his arms earlier, even for a few minutes, had filled him with a sense of peace he experienced only with her. He prayed he could convince her they both deserved some time away from the spy game and she'd let him whisk her away somewhere they could spend all day and night making love.

As he waited for the taxi, he closed his eyes and thought about the conversation he and Mercer had had with Quinn.

It had been brief, and her stated biggest concern was for her grandfather, which made Kade proud. Sensing she'd feel more comfortable talking with Mercer alone, he'd said goodbye, told her he loved her, and that he'd give her an update tomorrow with their travel plans.

Afterwards he'd realized Mercer would probably do the same; however, he had no intention of censoring the things he said to his daughter. He wanted an open and honest relationship with her.

Second only to Quinn was Merrigan. He'd thought about her every minute the medic had spent patching up his leg, and was determined not to hold back with her either. He wanted her to know how he felt, not just in the heat of the moment, but always. Everything he'd wanted to tell her in the last few weeks, he planned to tell her tonight.

He'd just exited the taxi in front of her building when a call came from Leech. The last thing he wanted was to have this conversation on a noisy London street, but he couldn't ignore it either. He looked around, but didn't see a quiet place he could duck into, either.

"Leech," he said, answering his phone. "I'm so sorry."

"As I told Paps, I don't blame him or you. Lena… my daughter…"

Even through the noise of the traffic swirling around him, Kade could hear the anguish in his mentor's voice. "I'm sorry," he said again. Simply unable to find the words to express his sorrow.

"Merrigan is good for you, Kade. Don't get caught up in feeling guilt over my daughter. You did more for her than anyone could've asked."

"I'm not feeling that way right now, Leech." Kade's eyes filled with the thought that he had failed her all those years ago. If only he'd stuck around long enough to realize the depth of her suffering.

"Stop it. I know what you're thinking, and I want you to let it go. I called to tell you that, while I don't hold you responsible for her death, I know you need my forgiveness anyway. You've got it, Doc. Now, forgive yourself."

After Leech disconnected the call, Kade stood outside Merrigan's building, processing what he'd said. For now, they were all still in shock. Lena's death hadn't really hit any of them yet. In the days and weeks to come, he knew he wouldn't be the only person searching his soul.

Before they'd exited the plane, Kade approached Razor when Paps stepped into the restroom.

"I'm worried about him."

"I am too."

"This isn't a typical…"

"I hear ya, Doc."

Razor agreed to keep an eye on the man who had been his best friend for almost twenty-five years. He'd told Kade he couldn't promise Paps would be in the mood for talking, but he knew how to be annoying enough to get him to have a few beers with him.

"When are we goin' home?" Razor asked.

Kade told him he hadn't figured it out yet, but not why. The next few days, hell, the next few years of his life, if he had his way, would be dependent on what Merrigan wanted to do.

He saw a car pull up and immediately recognized it as something MI6 would've ferried someone of Merrigan's level home in. When he saw her climb out with two children, one holding each hand, he smiled.

They'd spent hours talking about their families while he was a prisoner. Actually, he'd done most of the talking; she'd simply said she wasn't close to hers. Seeing her like this, surrounded by her people, warmed his heart because he knew how much it meant to her. It wasn't something she'd ever ask for, but she'd see it as a gift that her brother was making such an effort.

"Hi," she murmured, walking over to where he waited.

"Who's this?" he asked, looking down at her niece and nephew.

Merrigan shook her left hand. "This is Kevin, and on my right is Rowen."

Kade held out his hand, and Kevin shook it. "It's nice to meet you. My name is Doc."

A woman Kade assumed was Merrigan's sister-in-law was holding another little girl, who was trying to squirm out of her arms. He walked over to them.

"Hi," he said to the toddler. "Do you want to come see your Aunt Merrigan?"

"Oh, you're *good*. I'm Mary Pat, by the way," she said, attempting to let the little girl down. Instead, she reached out for Kade, who took her in his arms.

"I'm Doc."

"I'm Bronagh," she said and reached out for Merrigan.

"You two are going to have your hands full. I'm Mac," Merrigan's brother introduced himself.

"How so?" she asked.

Mac looked at Mary Pat, and they both laughed.

"What?" Merrigan asked.

"If I were a fortune teller, I'd see many wee ones on the horizon for you two."

Kade smiled and looked at Merrigan, whose cheeks had turned a deep shade of pink.

"By the way, Mer. I was sorry to hear about your mate."

"You mean Orlov?"

Mac nodded.

Kade could tell she was struggling with what to say, but finally admitted she was sorry too.

"Shall we go inside?" she asked, handing Bronagh back to Kade to look for her keys.

Mac laughed. "You're naturals."

"Watch it," she murmured. "I'm not above short-sheeting your bed."

"She used to do that to me all the bloody time." Mac chuckled. "I remember…"

Kade stopped listening to her brother's words and focused on two things only: the look of happiness on the face of the woman he loved and the little girl who rested her head on his chest, thumb in mouth. Quinn used to do that. He loved the way it felt to have her fall asleep snuggled up to him. He took a deep breath. There was nothing like the scent of a child. There was a pure sweetness that lasted only so long. He'd savored it with Quinn, not even realizing he had.

His eyes met Merrigan's. He could tell she was watching him. Her expression was both quizzical and happy. He hoped Mac's prediction was right. Nothing would make him happier than to hold their child in his arms.

31

Merrigan

She'd been trained to know how to react to many given situations, but this one had her baffled. Once they'd gone inside, Kade and her brother went about the flat, opening windows to air it out. Mary Pat had settled her nieces and nephew with books, then offered to help Merrigan in any way she could.

"I don't have much," Merrigan said. It had been months since she was home. "I should've thought about that on our way."

"What's that? I can run round to the store and pick up some groceries," Mac offered.

"I can go too," added Kade.

Merrigan scribbled a handful of things on a list, then handed it to Mary Pat.

"I wouldn't know where to begin," she said, looking over at the children.

"Mac's got it. Not to worry."

Before they left, Kade approached and kissed her soundly.

Mary Pat cleared her throat. "MacGregor Shaw, I faintly remember that you used to kiss me goodbye as well."

Merrigan laughed. This was all so normal and completely outside of her comfort zone. Could she even do normal? Had she ever? She couldn't remember a time when she had. Even as a little girl, her thoughts and dreams were so different from her schoolmates. While they'd talk about marrying the latest teen heartthrob, she'd dreamed about being Emma Peel.

"Are you holding up?" Mary Pat asked her once Kade and Mac had left.

"Yes…um…what do you mean?"

Her sister-in-law laughed. "You look a tinge shell-shocked."

"Just a tinge?" She laughed too. "Oh," she said, seeing a call coming in from Kade. "What'd you forget?" she asked.

"To tell you I love you. I never want to leave your side without saying those words to you."

Merrigan turned away from Mary Pat. "I love you too," she murmured. When he disconnected the call and she turned back around, her brother's wife was studying her.

"When Mac and I were first together, I think he was absolutely dumbfounded by how demonstrative my family was and, thus, me too."

Merrigan nodded, remembering how she'd been shocked by their public displays of affection when they had dinner together at the safe house.

"There's nothing wrong with it, you know."

"I do know. It's just…"

"You don't have to tell me." Mary Pat laughed again. "Your brother was as stiff-upper-lip as they come. Doc will loosen you up. I can see it already."

"Thank you," Merrigan said.

"Whatever for?"

"Making this so easy for me. I know I haven't been a part of your lives…"

Mary Pat grasped both her hands. "Maybe not in the flesh, but every night, our children beg for a story about their brilliantly adventurous Aunt Merrigan, star of every action-hero story their father can conjure up. And there have been some doozies. Ask him about the time you saved the world from the mad scientist who planned to make all the earth's volcanoes erupt simultaneously."

"Oh, goodness."

"You don't know the half. They all cheered when Aunt Merrigan pushed Doctor Lava into Mount Etna." Mary Pat smiled and shook her head. "Mac told you that Bronagh's middle name is Merrigan."

"Aye," she answered. "I was very emotional when he did."

"Did he also tell you that both Kevin and Rowen demanded to have their middle names changed to Merrigan as well?"

"You're kidding."

"I think Kev may have given up the cause now that he's in school and knows the ribbing he'd get from his mates. Rowen, however, I predict will have it legally changed as soon as she reaches eighteen. More so now that she's gotten to know you in person."

"Oh, dear. I hope I don't disappoint them."

"You never could," Mary Pat said. "That's what's so brilliant about children. Their love is absolutely unconditional. They haven't learned yet to be stingy with it, and if I have my way, they never will."

32

Kade

"I'm going to ask your sister to marry me," he blurted when he and Mac were less than halfway down the block.

"Yeah?"

Kade nodded.

"When?"

"Tonight."

"Right. Well, good. She loves you. You love her. No need to make it complicated. Let's see the ring."

The Ring. A ring. He'd completely forgotten that part.

Mac laughed. "Lucky for you, it's early." He pointed to a jeweler's shop across the way. "Just get her something simple, and she'll adore it."

"Uh…" Kade looked over at the shop window. "You think I should?"

"What? Get a ring? Don't be daft. You can't propose without a ring, mate. Come on. I'll help you choose."

Twenty minutes later, they walked out of the shop with a far more elaborate ring than Mac had initially suggested. As soon as Kade saw the diamond flanked by two sapphires, he knew that was the one.

"It'll match her eyes," he'd murmured.

When the jeweler asked Merrigan's ring size, Kade again was stumped.

"Six," said Mac. "Her fingers look about the same as Mary Pat's," he'd added once the jeweler walked away.

"So, you want us to clear out?"

"Actually, I have a room at Forty-Five Park Lane."

"Brilliant," Mac exclaimed, smiling and patting Kade on the back. "We'll get the kiddos squared away for bed, then you can whisk her away."

"You don't mind?"

"Hell, I haven't seen her for more than a couple hours in the last twenty years. Don't want to overdo it, ya know?"

"Did you stop for a pint?" Mary Pat teased when they finally returned to the flat.

Kade saw Merrigan catch her brother shush his wife before turning to him. "Did you?"

"We were bonding."

She laughed, and he loved the sound of it. It was only one of so many things he loved about the woman he'd known was an angel from the first time he saw her.

"I feel terrible just leaving," Merrigan said when they got in the taxi.

"He knew we wanted to have some time alone," Kade said, running his finger down her cheek and over her lips.

"You don't think it was rude, then?"

"That your brother practically pushed you out of your own apartment? No, not at all."

She smiled. "You soothe me, Kade."

"Do you have any idea how much I love you?" he asked, kissing her before she could respond.

When the taxi stopped in front of the hotel, Kade handed the driver a fistful of money and told him to keep the change.

He took Merrigan's hand in his. "I had a room at another hotel, but I really wanted to bring you here."

"It doesn't matter. We can—"

Kade cupped her chin and looked into her eyes. "But it does matter, Fatale. Everything matters tonight."

"The Imperial Penthouse," he said when they approached the front desk of the London's Mandarin Oriental.

Tonight would be the start of their life together, and Kade wanted everything to be perfect.

"What are you thinking?" he asked when he walked over to the elaborate vase of flowers she was admiring.

She smiled. "That it's perfect."

He beamed. "I love you."

"I love you, Kade."

33

Merrigan

Mary Pat had been right. The more she said aloud how she felt, the easier it was. Her heart pounded in the way it always did when Kade was near, and somehow, she knew that would never change. He'd always take her breath away, even without trying. And when he tried? He brought her to a precipice of pleasure she'd never known before and pushed her over, flying with her as she soared.

She longed to run her hands over the sculpted muscles of his lower abs she could picture so clearly when she closed her eyes, or her fingers over arms so powerful they strained the sleeves of his dress shirt.

Suddenly, Kade lunged at her and pushed her up against the side of the lift. "Whatever you're thinking, you have to stop. Just until we get to the room, baby. Because if you keep this up, I'm going to take you hard and fast right here, in this elevator."

His eyes, so blue against the chiseled lines of his face, bore into hers, and they both breathed a sigh of relief when the lift dinged, then opened directly into the luxurious penthouse.

"Merrigan." His sigh sounded almost prayer-like as they rushed to remove their clothes. Before she could take another breath, Kade stood before her, naked.

"I could spend hours looking at you," she murmured, running her hands over the tense muscles of his arms, then chest, then down to his hips.

Kade caught her hands in his and moved her toward the bed, so the backs of her legs were touching the king-size mattress. Then he pushed her so she was flat on her back, staring up at him. She parted her legs when he demanded her to, and watched as his eyes rested on her sex.

"You're ready for me, aren't you, Fatale?"

Her body writhed as she waited for him to stop looking and touch her. Finally, after what felt like minutes of him running his eyes over every inch of her, he thrust into her, making her gasp with the suddenness of feeling so full.

"You feel so good, baby," he whispered, leaning forward and rubbing the stubble on his cheek against her smooth skin. "I want to mark you, so every man who sees you knows I've made you mine. Are you mine, Fatale? All mine?"

"You know I am, Kade. I've never belonged to anyone but you."

He slowed then, moving in and out of her languidly, no longer frantic, no longer hurried. It was as though every stroke touched her in the perfect place to drive her wild, yet he refused to rush.

"Look at me," he said, and her eyes met his. "I want you to remember this moment forever, Merrigan. Right here, right now, I'm pledging myself to you for eternity and asking you to do the same."

Her eyes filled with tears, not with sadness or even joy, but with the surge of power she felt, knowing she would spend the rest of her life with Kade Butler.

"Marry me, Merrigan," he said, grasping the palms of her hands with his. "Spend your life with me, just like this, the two of us joined together whether our bodies are or not."

"Yes," she cried, determined not to hold anything back from the man who'd captured her heart and soul. "Marry me, Kade. Tonight. Tomorrow. I don't care. Just marry me."

With her words, he began thrusting into her again, harder than before. Within seconds, waves of pleasure so powerful she was breathless overtook her. Her body shuddered as though the core of her was the epicenter of a quake rippling through her, wave after wave.

His beautiful blue eyes filled with tears, like hers had, as he matched her explosion with his own. "I love you, Merrigan," he groaned as he spasmed inside of her, still thrusting, pounding out his pleasure.

He rested his body against hers, then rolled so she faced him. "I did it wrong," he murmured.

Merrigan's eyes scrunched. "I can assure you that you did it perfectly."

He smiled. "Not that." He rolled away from her. "Don't move," he said as he stood and left her lying in bed alone.

"No," she groaned, reaching for him. "Come back."

He leaned down and kissed her, thrusting his tongue into her mouth in the same way his body had thrust into hers only a minute ago. "I'll be right back," he whispered, touching her swollen lips with his fingertips.

She watched him walk over to where he'd tossed his jacket when they entered the penthouse. He picked it up and took something out of the pocket. The view of him walking back to her was equally devastating as watching the swagger of his perfect backside. There was power in every step he took, unmatched by any other human being she'd known.

"Come here," he said, taking her arm and pulling her so she sat at the side of the bed and dangled her legs in front of him.

He leaned forward so the muscles of his chest touched her legs, and took her hand in his. "I've already asked you once tonight, but I'll do it right this time."

Merrigan watched as he slid the ring on her finger.

"Marry me, Merrigan. Make me whole."

"Yes, I'll marry you," she said, throwing her arms around him. No ring, no piece of jewelry he could give her would outweigh his simple words of love, but she pulled back to study its beauty.

"It's gorgeous," she breathed.

"It fits," he said, smiling and moving the ring just slightly on her finger.

"Perfectly," she answered. "Just like we do."

Epilogue

Kade couldn't remember a time when he'd ever felt as nervous as he did today. Whatever the outcome, it didn't matter to him, but how it would affect the precious woman standing in front of him did.

With Mercer by her side, Quinn opened the envelope. He so wished she hadn't felt the need to do this. He'd told her time and again that nothing any piece of paper said would change the love he felt for her, but she'd insisted.

"I have to know," she'd said, and he was powerless to deny her.

This was her decision, and he understood her desire for the truth.

He watched her pull the paper from the envelope. Time felt as though it was standing still as he waited for her to unfold and read it.

When her eyes filled with tears and spilled out onto her cheeks, Kade froze in panic.

"I knew it," she said, smiling up at him. "But you needed to know it too."

She handed him the piece of paper, and there it was. The proof he'd been too afraid to hope for. Quinn was his daughter in every way. There wasn't a single cell in her body that had come from evil. Every bit of her was filled with nothing but love.

Mercer walked over to the sliding door that opened to the patio and waved to Merrigan, Paps, and Razor. Meanwhile, Kade opened the bottle of champagne that had been chilling in the refrigerator and poured five glasses, plus one glass of water.

When Merrigan came inside, her eyes met his, questioning, and he smiled. He looked over at Quinn, and his beloved did the same. She smiled too as she walked into his arms.

"I'm so happy for you both," she whispered.

"Thank you, sweetheart." He leaned down and kissed her softly, then pulled back to look in her eyes once more. "Everything I've ever wanted in life is right here in front of me."

He rested his hand on her belly. Merrigan was six months pregnant, and the two of them had endured plenty of ribbing for it. Everyone teased that he'd gotten her that way only moments after they were married in a quiet ceremony the day after he'd proposed, with only her brother and his family, along with the minister joining them. Once they'd arrived back in the States, they'd had a second ceremony and subsequent celebration with his family.

"I'd like to propose a toast," he said and waited for everyone to raise their glasses. "To Quinn Analise Butler, within hours to be Bryant, my stunningly beautiful, staggeringly smart, flesh-of-my-flesh daughter."

"I still can't believe you wanted to do this today," Razor said to him quietly.

"It wasn't my decision," Kade answered. "She wanted to know before the wedding tomorrow."

"Man, what if it had gone the other way?"

Kade had spent many hours worrying that it would, but it hadn't, and that was all that mattered.

"I just thank God it didn't."

"I hear ya. Hey, mind if I make a toast of my own?" Razor asked.

"Go right ahead."

"Raise your glasses one more time," he began. "I'd like to make a toast to the men and women"—he paused and looked at Merrigan—"of K19 Security

Solutions. Brothers and sisters in arms. To us—Kade, Gunner, Mercer, Merrigan, and me—and to those who will soon join us in saving the world."

They all drank to his toast, but only Kade heard the whispered words Razor added. "And to tomorrow, when my life irrevocably changes forever."

Keep reading for a sneak peek
at the first book in the
K19 Security Solutions Team One series,
Razor's Edge

He's a deadly operative. She's his high-stakes assignment.
Together, they'll face a threat neither saw coming.
In a world of danger, their love might
be the riskiest move of all.

RAZOR

I never expected to fall in love on an assignment, but Avarie McNamara changed everything. She's beautiful, smart, and in more danger than she knows. As I fight to keep her safe from her own father—a man I've been hunting for years—I realize I can't imagine my life without her. But with enemies closing in, can I protect the woman I love and bring down one of the world's most dangerous men?

AVA

When Tabon "Razor" Sharp came into my life, I thought he was just another hot guy. I had no idea he'd turn my world upside down. Now I'm on the run from my father, falling hard for the man protecting me, and questioning everything I thought I knew. Razor makes me feel safe in a world full of danger, but can our love survive the secrets and lies surrounding us?

1

Razor

"What the hell are you doin' now?" Gunner asked.

Truth was, he was standing in front of a mirror, giving himself a pep talk. It wasn't being a groomsman in their mutual friend's wedding that worried him, or even that K19 Security Solutions—the company he and Gunner owned with two other partners—was morphing so quickly he hardly recognized it anymore. Instead, it was the woman his friend's fiancée had paired him up with in the wedding party.

Avarie McNamara, who he should've forgotten months ago, wound up center stage in every fantasy he had when he needed to take the edge off. It didn't help that the one and only time he'd met her in person, she was wearing the hottest damn bikini he'd ever seen.

She'd let him know, in no uncertain terms, that she was interested that day, but he hadn't been able to take her up on it. He'd been on the clock, filling in as her friend's bodyguard long before she knew she had one.

He'd known a lot about Ava prior to her coming on to him that day, but he hadn't allowed himself to get to know her in the intimate way she was suggesting.

"It's a damn tuxedo," Gunner griped, interrupting his thoughts of the gorgeous woman he was about to see for the first time in over a year. "There's one way to wear it. Nobody gives a shit what you look like, anyway. Let's go."

It wasn't unusual for Gunner to be grouchy—that's just the way the guy was.

"What is with you?" Gunner asked when they got in the car.

"I don't want to talk about it."

Gunner shot him a look.

"Ava McNamara," Razor admitted, rolling his shoulders.

"Hot little number. Her twin too. How is she a problem?"

"I can't stop thinking about her."

"Not like you," Gunner muttered.

"You should've seen the bikini she had on, that day on Fire Island."

He'd spent a total of twenty minutes with her, so for her to be on his mind at all was unusual.

But the fantasies? Shit. There were times they seemed so real he could swear he knew exactly how her nipples would harden under his touch, and how her wetness would coat his fingers when he sneaked them in her bikini bottom.

He could even remember how she'd smelled that day. At first it was of sand and sun and margaritas, but the longer they'd talked, the more the sweet scent of her arousal eclipsed everything else. That wasn't something he had to imagine; that was a bona fide memory.

If Ava was wearing the same dress Penelope was, those fantasies he'd been having would soon get a hell of a lot hotter.

The small amount of pale green fabric she wore was shorter than most bridesmaids' dresses he'd seen, with a halter top that left little to the imagination. Ava and her sister, Aine, were far more endowed than this girl. He couldn't even imagine how good the dress would look on them.

Gunner laughed. "You're in for it."

He knew it, but then there was always a chance that reality-Ava wouldn't be half as hot as he remembered her being. Unfortunately it was the opposite. She was twice as hot, and if he didn't get myself into her tight little body tonight, he'd be able to pound nails with the raging hard-on he got every time her image crept into his brain.

About the Author

USA Today best-selling author Heather Slade writes shamelessly sexy, edge-of-your seat romantic suspense.

She gave herself the gift of writing a book for her own birthday one year. Sixty-plus books later (and counting), she's having the time of her life.

The women Slade writes are self-confident, strong, with wills of their own, and hearts as big as the Colorado sky. The men are sublimely sexy, seductive alphas who rise to the challenge of capturing the sweet soul of a woman whose heart they'll hold in the palm of their hand forever. Add in a couple of neck-snapping twists and turns, a page-turning mystery, and a swoon-worthy HEA, and you'll be holding one of her books in your hands.

She loves to hear from her readers. You can contact her at heather@heatherslade.com

To keep up with her latest news and releases, please visit her website at www.heatherslade.com to sign up for her newsletter.

MORE FROM AUTHOR HEATHER SLADE

ROMANTIC SUSPENSE

K19 SECURITY SOLUTIONS TEAM ONE
Razor's Edge
Gunner's Redemption
Mistletoe's Magic
Mantis' Desire
Dutch's Salvation

K19 SECURITY SOLUTIONS TEAM TWO
Striker's Choice
Monk's Fire
Halo's Oath
Tackle's Honor
Onyx's Awakening

K19 SHADOW OPERATIONS TEAM ONE
Code Name: Ranger
Code Name: Diesel
Code Name: Wasp
Code Name: Cowboy
Code Name: Mayhem

K19 ALLIED INTELLIGENCE TEAM ONE
Code Name: Ares
Code Name: Cayman
Code Name: Poseidon
Code Name: Zeppelin
Code Name: Magnet

K19 ALLIED INTELLIGENCE TEAM TWO
Code Name: Puck
Code Name: Michelangelo
Code Name: Typhon
Code Name: Hornet
Code Name: Reaper

K19 GENESIS CONSORTIUM TEAM ONE
Blackjack's Ascent
Dagger's Shield
Sundance's Trail
Nomad's Compass
Preacher's Decree

K19 SENTINEL CYBER TEAM ONE
Code Name: Admiral
Code Name: Dante
Code Name: Grit
Code Name: Tank
Code Name: Atticus

K19 SENTINEL CYBER TEAM TWO
Code Name: Kodiak
Code Name: Paragon
Code Name: Vex
Code Name: Shredder
Code Name: Jagger

PROTECTORS UNDERCOVER TEAM ONE
Undercover Agent
Undercover Emissary
Undercover Savior
Undercover Infidel
Undercover Shadow

ROYAL AGENTS OF MI6
Make Me Shiver
Drive Me Wilder
Feel My Pinch
Chase My Shadow
Find My Angel

THE INVINCIBLES TEAM ONE
Code Name: Deck
Code Name: Edge
Code Name: Grinder
Code Name: Rile
Code Name: Smoke

THE INVINCIBLES TEAM TWO
Code Name: Buck
Code Name: Irish
Code Name: Saint
Code Name: Hammer
Code Name: Rip

THE UNSTOPPABLES TEAM ONE
Code Name: Fury
Code Name: Merried

MORE FROM AUTHOR HEATHER SLADE

WINE COUNTRY ROMANCE

BUTLER RANCH
Kade's Worth
Brodie's Promise
Maddox's Truce
Naughton's Secret
Mercer's Vow
Kade's Return
Butler Ranch Christmas

WICKED WINEMAKERS
CENTRAL COAST
FIRST LABEL
Brix's Bid
Ridge's Release
Press' Passion
Zin's Sins
Tryst's Temptation

WICKED WINEMAKERS
CENTRAL COAST
SECOND LABEL
Beau's Beloved
Cru's Crush
Bit's Bliss
Snapper's Seduction
Kick's Kiss

WICKED WINEMAKERS
RUSSIAN RIVER VALLEY
FIRST LABEL
Bas' Blend
Hux's Harvest
Wolf's Want
Oak's Vintage
Cooper's Claim

COWBOY ROMANCE

COWBOYS OF
CRESTED BUTTE
A Cowboy Falls
A Cowboy's Dance
A Cowboy's Kiss
A Cowboy Stays
A Cowboy Wins

ROARING FORK RANCH
Roaring Fork Wrangler
Roaring Fork Roughstock
Roaring Fork Rockstar
Roaring Fork Rooker
Roaring Fork Bridger

SANGRE VISTA RANCH
Thorn's Stand
Stetson's Storm
Maverick's Reckoning
Cinch's Wager
Flints Chance